W9-AYK-851

# Close Your Eyes

## ROBIN JONES GUNN

## BETHANY HOUSE PUBLISHERS
MINNEAPOLIS, MINNESOTA 55438

Focus on the Family books are available at special quantity discounts when purchased in bulk by corporations, organizations, churches, or groups. Special imprints, messages, and excerpts can be produced to meet your needs. For more information, contact: Focus on the Family Sales Department,
8605 Explorer Drive, Colorado Springs, CO 80920; or phone (800) 932-9123.

A Focus on the Family book published by
Bethany House Publishers
11400 Hampshire Avenue South
Bloomington, Minnesota 55438
www.bethanyhouse.com

Bethany House Publishers is a Division of
Baker Book House Company, Grand Rapids, Michigan.

Printed in the United States of America

**Library of Congress Cataloging-in-Publication Data**
Gunn, Robin Jones, 1955–
  Close your eyes / Robin Jones Gunn.
    p.  cm. — (The Sierra Jensen series ; #4)
  Summary: When Sierra volunteers to help at a local homeless shelter, she finds herself much more involved than she planned, especially when Paul shows up there as a staff worker.
    ISBN 1–56179–487–2
    [1. Christian life—Fiction.]  I. Title.
  II. Series: Gunn, Robin Jones, 1955–    Sierra Jensen series ; #4
  PZ7.G972Cl    1996                                           96–20938
                                                                    CIP
                                                                    AC

04   05   06   07   08   09   /   20   19   18   17   16   15   14   13   12

For Janet Kobobel Grant

This is our twentieth book together, my friend.
May our readers know what I've known
all along—I could never have done
them without you.

# From Robin Jones Gunn

## THE CHRISTY MILLER SERIES

## CHRISTY & TODD: THE COLLEGE YEARS

## THE SIERRA JENSEN SERIES

# chapter one

"**H**OW COME THIS STUFF MAKES SENSE TO you?" Randy Jenkins asked, tossing his wadded-up gum wrapper into the fireplace. A high school physics book lay propped like a tent on the floor in front of him, and half a dozen papers surrounded him.

Sierra pushed the painted enamel bracelet up her arm and cast her buddy an encouraging smile. "You almost have it," she said. "Give it one more try."

While Randy fussed over his homework, Sierra stretched out her legs and fondly gazed around the warm family room. The grand Victorian house, which had been in her family for more than 50 years, offered plenty of space.

Sierra tilted her head and tried to catch Randy's gaze with her gray-blue eyes. "You want to take a break and eat something?"

Before Randy could answer, Sierra's older sister, Tawni, burst into the room clutching the remote phone in her drooping hand. "Where's Mom?"

"She took the boys to get haircuts." Sierra noticed tears glistening in Tawni's eyes. If Sierra guessed right, Tawni had been talking to her new boyfriend, Jeremy Mackenzie, as she usually did this time of day, every day. Conversations with Jeremy were prone to cause smiles and whispers, not tears.

"Are you okay?" Sierra asked cautiously. She and her sister had never been exceptionally close and such a question could embarrass Tawni, especially since Randy was there.

"Sure. Fine. I'm going to make cookies," Tawni announced and marched through the family room into the kitchen.

"Now I know she's upset," Sierra said in a low voice to Randy.

He was scratching a list of figures on a piece of notebook paper and didn't look up.

"Something happened between her and Jeremy. I bet he's not coming."

"What?" Randy said, looking up. His straight, dark-blond hair, which was cut in what Sierra's Granna Mae called a "Dutch boy," fell into his eyes. "Were you talking to me?"

"Never mind," Sierra said. Gathering her long gauze skirt in her hand, she stood up and headed for the kitchen. "I'll be right back."

"Whatever," Randy muttered.

The counter was already covered with all the dry-goods canisters from the pantry, including one filled with pasta. Two eggs sat precariously close to the edge of the counter, and a large bottle of vanilla extract stood with its lid off, spreading its pleasant fragrance like a blessing over the baking event. Tawni was smearing butter on two cookie sheets as Sierra entered. Her sister didn't look up but dumped the rest of the butter stick into a mixing bowl and furiously began to chop at it with a wooden spoon.

"Are you all right?" Sierra asked again.

"Of course I am! Just because Jeremy isn't coming to see me this weekend after all our planning doesn't mean my life should come to a standstill. I have lots to do. Lots and lots!"

"Why isn't he coming?"

"Money, school, finals. Take your pick."

Sierra lowered herself onto a kitchen stool and felt her heart sinking. During the weeks Tawni and Jeremy had been planning his visit from San Diego, Sierra had been busy secretly making her own wishes. Jeremy had a brother, Paul, whom Sierra had happened to meet at the airport in London five months ago. Since then she had seen him around town twice and received two letters from him. Their brief conversations and correspondence had left Sierra with a treasure chest full of "what if's" buried deep inside her heart.

When she had found out Paul and Jeremy were brothers, it seemed inevitable her path would cross with Paul's. Then when Jeremy decided to come to Portland to see Tawni, Sierra had known her treasure chest was about to be opened. But now all those possibilities were crushed.

"So, is he going to come later? After school is out?"

"He's going to try." Tawni opened the cupboard door and began to move the spices around. "Where does Mom hide the chocolate chips?"

"In the pantry," Sierra said. "On the top shelf behind the paper towels."

Tawni went to the pantry and continued her search as Sierra tried to rearrange the dreams in her treasure chest.

"That's not so bad," she told Tawni (and herself). "Only a few more weeks. Besides, in June, Jeremy should be able to stay longer. This weekend would have been here and gone like that." Sierra snapped her fingers for emphasis. "Don't you think it will be much better if he comes for a whole week?"

"I guess. That is, of course, if he can pull together the money by then. His car needs new brakes, and his bank account is shot."

"Probably from paying his phone bill," Sierra muttered.

"What is that supposed to mean?" Tawni spun around with a roll of paper towels in her hand.

Sierra should have known better than to challenge Tawni when she was in such a mood—especially because, at 18, Tawni didn't put much value in Sierra's 16-year-old logic. But she spoke up anyway.

"You guys talk constantly on the phone. I'm sure it adds up. Neither of you has that much money. It doesn't make sense to me. Why don't you save some money by not calling each other all the time?"

"Sierra," Tawni said, shelving the paper towels, "you don't know the first thing about love!"

"You're right. I don't."

Surprised by Sierra's admission, Tawni didn't respond but continued her search for the chocolate chips.

"I guess love makes you do crazy things," Sierra said. "Like spending all your money on a phone bill instead of a plane ticket."

Tawni pursed her lips together as if she were holding back a flood of words.

"It was only a suggestion," Sierra mumbled, holding up her hands in surrender.

*You're not the only one affected by this, Tawni,* she thought. *All my dreams of seeing Paul are dissolved now, too, you know.* Of course, Sierra would never admit that to her sister.

A stiff silence crowded the large kitchen as Tawni reached her arm into the dark recesses of the cupboard above the refrigerator. "Aha! Perfect!" She extracted a large, crumpled bag of M&M's.

"Those look like they've been in there for a decade," Sierra said.

"So? The bag is still closed. Don't they put enough preservatives in these things to keep them fresh into the next century?" Tawni pulled open the bag with a snap and poured the candy onto the counter. "Go ahead. Try one," she challenged.

"I'm not going to try one," Sierra said. "You try one."

It occurred to Sierra that she and her sister had

somehow changed roles. All their lives, Sierra had been the daring, rambunctious one even though she was younger. When they were little, Tawni was the dainty, prissy one who insisted on using a straw to drink her milk lest she fall prey to a dreaded milk mustache.

Now Tawni was acting like Sierra by turning the kitchen into a war zone in her attempt to make cookies, and Sierra had turned into Miss Finicky. Funny how she would go against her true nature just to oppose her sister.

"Oh, this is crazy," Sierra spouted, grabbing a handful of M&M's. "Look, I'm eating them." She tossed them into her mouth just as Randy entered the kitchen.

"What's happening?" he asked.

"I'm making cookies," Tawni said. "And Sierra is acting like her stubborn self."

"I am not," Sierra said, her words coming out garbled through the M&M's.

It wasn't unusual for Randy to hear this kind of banter, which frequently flew between Sierra and Tawni. About three weeks ago, he had started to stop by Sierra's house regularly. At first it was on Friday nights, then it was Mondays, Wednesdays, Fridays, and any other night he wasn't working at his lawn-care business. He even came by one night and had dinner with Sierra's family when Sierra was at her friend Amy Degrassi's house. Sierra's parents encouraged "drop-by" friendships, so Randy had quickly become a part of the family.

"I have only one question," Randy said, sitting next to Sierra and nudging the two eggs away from the edge of the counter. "When will they be ready?"

"Soon," Tawni said, measuring the sugar and double-checking to make sure it was exactly right.

"Let us know when you're ready for taste testers," Randy said, heading back to the family room. "I have to finish this homework tonight."

"Me, too," Sierra said. She gave Tawni a pleasant look and added, "Just keep telling yourself it will only be a few more weeks before he comes."

Tawni looked surprised and tossed back an amiable "Yeah, well, thanks for caring."

*Oh, I do!* Sierra thought. *More than you know, dear sis. More than you know!*

# chapter two

"**I** **THINK I CLOBBERED THE LAST TWO PROBLEMS.** Only one more to go," Randy said. "I sure will be glad when school's out."

"Me, too," Sierra said, hiding a smile that was tied to her dreams of seeing Paul once school ended.

The phone rang, and a moment later Tawni called from the kitchen, "Sierra, it's Amy."

"I'll take it in the study," Sierra told Randy. "Call me if you get stuck."

She hopped up and hurried into the library, her favorite room in the rambling, old house. Curling up in the chair by the French doors that led to the backyard, Sierra reached for the phone and punched the On button.

"Hi, Aimers!" Sierra heard the click as her sister hung up the kitchen extension.

"Is Randy over there?" Amy asked.

"Yes, he's in the family room finishing up the physics problems. Have you done yours yet?"

"Are you kidding? It's not due until Friday. And why do you always change the subject when I mention Randy?"

"I did not change the subject. However, I do have news for you."

"What?"

"Guess."

"I give up."

"You give up too easily, Amy."

"I know I do. Is that why you called? To harass me about being an underachiever?"

"I didn't call you. You called me."

"Oh, that's right. Tell me your news quick, and then I'll tell you mine."

"Jeremy's not coming."

"And that means you won't get to see Paul, right?"

"Right."

"Bummer," Amy said.

"I know." Sierra let out a sigh. "I shouldn't be so obsessed with the thought of seeing this guy, but . . ."

"But you can't keep yourself from demonstrating a common characteristic of the obsessive-compulsive person. You won't be happy until you get what you want, and then when you get it, you won't be happy because the fantasy will be over."

"Oh please, Dr. Degrassi, stop with the psycho-analyzing. I am not an obsessive-compulsive person, and you know it."

"Okay, then you're lost in a fantasy."

"It's not that either."

"Then, what is it?" Amy challenged.

"I don't know. It's just that Paul is . . ."

"Unattainable?"

"Not necessarily."

"Can I tell you what I think?" Amy asked. Sierra could picture her dark-eyed friend sprawled on her patchwork bedspread, flipping back her long, curly black hair as she prepared to dispense pearls of wisdom.

"From what you've told me about Paul, I'd say drop the dream right now and pay attention to Randy. You know he likes you. Paul is nothing more than a phantom, a mysterious stranger whose life momentarily intersected with yours. That's all. You both now spin in separate orbits, and it's not meant for you to share each other's paths at this time."

Sierra burst out laughing. "Where do you come up with this sci-fi psychiatry? I don't like it when you talk creepy like that."

"That's not creepy. That's poetic," Amy said.

"It sounds as if you're giving coordinates for the space shuttle, not talking about real people. Paul is a real person. He's not a phantom."

"All I'm saying, Sierra, is there's no point in wishing for something that's not going to happen when something great is waiting around the corner for you."

Sierra didn't answer.

"Okay, to be more accurate—when something great is waiting for you in the family room."

"Randy and I are buddies," Sierra said. "You know that. Why are you suddenly so interested in directing my social life?"

"Because," Amy began, "I have a great idea. That's why I called. Why don't we fix dinner for a couple of the guys as an end-of-school party? My mom said we could do it over here. We could get a couple of lobsters from my uncle's restaurant and make it really fancy."

"Sounds fun," Sierra said. "When do you want to do it?"

"I don't know. Maybe next Friday."

"And who are you going to invite?" Sierra asked. "Drake?"

"Yes, that is, if he happens to acknowledge my existence this week. You'll invite Randy, of course."

Sierra didn't answer right away. She twisted her finger around one of her long, blond curls and noticed that she needed to wash her hair. Too much de-frizzer this morning had made it feel sticky.

"Sierra," Amy repeated, "you will invite Randy, won't you?"

"Maybe."

"Oh, no! You're not off with that phantom in your head again, are you?"

"Maybe," Sierra answered, with a lilt in her voice. The really fun thing about Paul was that the more she had thought about him the last few months, the more she had convinced herself she had a crush on him. No, more than that, she and Paul were brought together by God, and she just knew that something had to happen between them—hopefully, very soon.

"Okay, Sierra," Amy said, "try to let that brainy little

head of yours grasp the full meaning of this poetic statement: 'A Randy in the hand is worth two Pauls in the bush.'"

"If you say so, Amy." Sierra knew the best route to take was to give in. She could be agreeable on the outside, but nobody could unlock that treasure chest of dreams she had hidden inside her heart.

## chapter three

"**T**HESE AREN'T BAD," SIERRA SAID, BITING into one of Tawni's cookies the next day at lunch. "You want one? My sister made them yesterday."

Amy pushed aside her cafeteria tray with her cold fries and half-eaten hamburger sprawled across the plate, revealing its three layers: bun, meat, bun. Amy was a finicky eater—when she ate.

Amy nibbled at the cookie Sierra handed her and was about to give her opinion when Drake appeared behind her and said, "It's not going to bite you back, Miss Amy!" He sandwiched himself between Amy and Sierra and made himself at home.

Drake's whole name was Anton Francisco Drake. Everyone knew that. And everyone simply called him "Drake"—even the teachers. He wore his dark hair combed straight back and stuck out his jaw whenever he tried to emphatically make a point about something. At six foot two and as one of the school's star athletes, Drake had little difficulty making whatever point he wanted to.

Right now, he was eyeing Sierra's cookies.

"You want one?" Sierra offered.

"Sure." Drake inhaled it in one bite. "You make them?"

"No, my sister did. She was in a strange mood yesterday afternoon and baked herself silly."

"You guys want to go to the Blazers game this Friday? A bunch of us are. You can still get tickets if you want to go with us," Drake said.

"I'd love to," Amy said. "Basketball is one of my favorite sports."

Randy tapped Sierra's arm and said, "Are you going?"

"I don't think so. I'm trying to save up some money."

"You want to go, Randy?" Drake asked.

"Maybe. I'll let you know."

Drake picked at the uneaten fries on Amy's tray and said, "Let me know if you want a ride."

"I do," Amy said quickly.

It seemed to Sierra that, for the first time, Drake was catching on. He seemed to realize that Amy was interested in him. His expression lightened a bit as he grabbed a few more of her cold fries. "Better draw me a map," he said. "I don't think I've ever been to your house."

"No, you haven't," Amy answered sweetly. She glanced at Sierra and winked—her way of secretly signaling victory. "I'll draw a map for you today," Amy said to Drake. "What time do you want me to be ready?"

Drake gave his broad shoulders a casual shrug. "Around 6:30, I guess."

"Sounds great," Amy said.

The bell rang, and the six people sitting at their table all rose and cleared their trays. The others went on ahead as Amy hung back, clasping Sierra's arm.

"Can you believe it?" she whispered to Sierra, her dark eyes aglow. "Drake finally asked me out!"

"Yeah, with a little help from you," Sierra teased.

"This is so perfect! We can start planning our nice dinner for the following Friday. I'm so excited!"

Amy didn't need to tell Sierra she was elated. It showed all over her face. She continued to ramble on with plans for their dinner as they headed for class.

*What a contrast this friend of mine can be!* Sierra thought. Sometimes Amy carried with her all the maturity and wisdom of the ages, wisdom that she gladly spewed, with or without an invitation to do so. The youngest of three girls, Amy had gathered many insights from her older sisters. Other times, like now, she was every bit the baby of the family, set on getting her way and sweetly finagling the situation to make sure that's what happened.

The two girls took their seats next to each other in class, and Amy leaned over to give Sierra her opinion. "Why don't you go to the game with Randy? The four of us could go out afterward. Come on, Sierra!"

Sierra shook her head, her wild curls chasing each other across her shoulders. "I already have a date with my civics book."

"You do not. You already finished that chapter. You

told me so yourself."

"There's always the extra-credit questions, you know."

Amy rolled her eyes and shook her head. "You drive me crazy. You know that? You absolutely drive me crazy. Maybe Vicki and Mike will want to go with Drake and me."

"Probably," Sierra said.

"Okay, class," Mr. Rykert called over the rumbling of conversations. "Take out your assignments and pass them forward, please."

Sierra gave Amy her final thought on Friday night. "I hope you and Drake have the time of your lives!"

Amy flashed an appreciative smile. She looked like a little girl when she smiled like that—timid, yet with a crazy exuberance. Sierra liked that about her. It was part of their common ground.

Handing in her paper, Sierra tried to keep her eyes and her mind from wandering to the back of the classroom where Randy sat behind Vicki Navarone.

*Relationships are such illusive things. First Tawni and her lovesick groanings over Jeremy. Now Amy and her overly eager attention toward Drake. And what's my problem? My brain is stuck on Paul. Am I only deluding myself that anything could ever happen there? And why is Amy so convinced that Randy likes me as more than a pal?*

She glanced back and noticed Randy and Vicki chatting away like old chums. *See? Randy is friends with a bunch of girls. I'm one of his many buddies, that's all.*

Randy and Vicki had gone out once, but nothing

seemed to develop after that—additional evidence that he was pal material and nothing more.

"Okay, class. Let's open in prayer," Mr. Rykert said.

In Sierra's opinion, this had to be one of the advantages of going to a small Christian high school. Even though most teachers prayed only in their first-period classes, Mr. Rykert always led them in prayer in his class. Sierra loved to hear him talk to God. He prayed as if God were standing right there in the room with them.

Sierra silently formed her own prayer that her mind wouldn't be so full of thoughts about guys. She prayed she would be able to finish the next few weeks of her junior year with the best grades she could get. Her older brother Wes had been pelting her lately with a barrage of information on college scholarships and awards. Sierra had the smarts to qualify for a lot of the programs, but this was the first semester she had thought seriously about college.

"Amen," Mr. Rykert concluded. Raising his voice, he announced, "This year for your final, I've prepared something a little different. You'll be writing a paper on a personal experience and presenting it to the class during the last week of school."

*Sounds easy,* Sierra thought. *I'll write about the outreach trip I took to England last January. Or maybe I'll write about what it's like to live with an aging grandmother and how my Granna Mae had surgery a few months ago.*

"And," Mr. Rykert continued, "I'm going to assign each of you a partner."

Amy and Sierra exchanged glances. Drake wasn't in

this class, so it was likely Amy would want to pair up with
Sierra. For a brief moment, Sierra thought it would be fun
to partner with Randy.

"I will explain the assignment for your final and then
tell you who your partner will be," Mr. Rykert said. "I
have a list of agencies here in Portland that accept volunteer assistance. Each of you, as a team, will select one of the
organizations on the list. No duplicates, please. You and
your partner will contact your organization and go
together to volunteer your assistance for a minimum of
four hours. You will then prepare a report and give it in
front of the class."

"Can we choose our own partners?" Amy asked.

"No, I will assign them. And no changes, please. What
I'm passing out now is a list of the organizations, a list of
the partners, and a list of the information you must
include in your report. Any other questions?"

"When is this due?" Amy asked.

"You have two weeks to complete the four hours of
service, and the written and oral reports are both due
finals week. It's on the bottom page."

Sierra took the papers from the guy ahead of her and
passed the stack to the girl behind her.

A girl in the front let out a mock groan and said, "Not
Jonah! Please give me anybody but Jonah."

"Thanks a lot," Jonah said. "At least I have a car, and
you don't. If you're real nice, I might even let you pay for
the gas."

"Byron Davis!" Amy whispered loud enough for only

Sierra to hear. Her face lit up as she leaned closer. "Are all my dreams coming true today or what?"

Byron, the strong, silent, studious type, sat two seats up. He was a straight-A student, and being partnered with him almost certainly guaranteed Amy an A on this final. Byron was studying the list of organizations and apparently hadn't checked to see who his partner was. Or maybe he hadn't mustered the courage. Byron gave the impression, because he was shy, that he was afraid of girls.

Sierra wouldn't have minded a bit if Byron had been her assigned partner. They would earn an A for sure. And she wouldn't be caught in that awkward trap of always feeling like she was the smart one.

Before Sierra could force herself to turn the page, she heard Randy call out, "Hey, Sierra!"

She turned around to see Randy holding up his paper and smiling. "It's you and me—Jensen and Jenkins. We're going to ace this final, buddy!"

Sierra gave him a thumbs-up signal and turned back around. Amy caught her eye and gave her a knowing look. With a delicate lift of her dark eyebrow, Amy mouthed the name "Randy" and smiled coyly at Sierra.

# chapter four

S IERRA IGNORED AMY AND LOOKED OVER THE papers that had been passed out. The rest of the class time was spent reviewing the chapter in the textbook. When the bell rang, Sierra tossed her papers into her backpack and was about to leave when Mr. Rykert called her and Randy up to the front.

They stood together by his desk as Mr. Rykert waited until the rest of the class cleared out. "You probably noticed," he began, "that the partners were selected alphabetically. I considered changing it so that you," he nodded toward Sierra, "would be partnered with Tre."

She hoped the sudden twitch she felt didn't show on her face. Tre Nuygen had transferred into the class mid-semester and was either the shyest student in the whole school or didn't speak English well enough to fit in. Amy said he came from Cambodia and had arrived in the United States only a few months ago. Someone else said he had been kicked out of the public high school, and Royal Christian Academy was the only school in Portland that would let him in.

Whatever the case, Tre was not a desirable partner, and Vicki had ended up being matched with him.

"I have a question for you two," Mr. Rykert said. "Would you be willing to work as a foursome with Vicki and Tre?"

"Sure," Randy said with a casual shrug of his shoulders.

"Sure," Sierra said after a slight pause. "That would be fine."

"Mr. Rykert?" a voice called from the back of the classroom. Vicki stood by the open door. Worry ripples creased her forehead and gathered above her clear green eyes. Vicki had learned to use her good looks and popularity to her advantage.

"Come in, Vicki," Mr. Rykert said. "We were talking about you. I'd like you and Tre to partner with Sierra and Randy."

"Oh, thank you," she said, including Randy and Sierra in her gracious, sweeping glance. "I feel much better about that."

"And may I suggest the location?" Mr. Rykert said. "I'd like the four of you to go to the Highland House. They run several services for the homeless and low-income families. You'll be volunteering with the after-school Kids Klub. It's run by the Highland Outreach Ministries. Do you know where it's located?"

"It's not far from where I work," Sierra said. "I've seen it, but I didn't know what it was."

"The main goal of the Highland House is to get people

back on their feet. They run a limited job referral service and offer some career training programs. The Kids Klub is for children whose parents are working. These kids would be on the streets otherwise, since many of them literally have no home. Others live in places that would be unsafe for them to go home to alone."

"There are kids like that in our city?" Randy said.

"More than you would guess," Mr. Rykert replied.

"This ought to be an education," Sierra said.

"That's what I'm counting on. So," Mr. Rykert said, rubbing his hands together and giving the three of them a warm look of assurance, "you're all set. Randy, you tell Tre what's going on, okay?"

"Okay."

"Let me know if you have any questions."

"Thanks, Mr. Rykert," Vicki said. She turned to Randy and gave him a puppy-dog look loaded with appreciation. "I feel so much better about this."

Something began to simmer inside of Sierra. Why was she feeling this way? Hadn't she prayed about her feelings toward Randy less than an hour ago? Why was it that one hint of flirtation from Vicki made Sierra feel she needed to protect Randy? Or flirt back with him or something?

She hurried to her next class, asking God why things like this were beginning to bother her so much. It made her feel so immature. The teasing from Amy and the twinges of jealousy over Vicki were experiences Sierra wasn't used to. Why was God opening the floodgate of testing situations? Was He trying to see if she really meant what she prayed?

Slipping into her seat in her next class, Sierra thought about Vicki and tried to be fair. Sierra knew if she had been matched with Tre, she would have wanted Mr. Rykert to do exactly what he did.

*Besides,* she chided herself, *this isn't about relationships. This is about school. It's about getting an A on the final. That's all. That's the most important thing for me right now. And if this check on my emotions is some kind of final from You, God, I want to get an A on that, too.*

That evening, as Sierra was leaving her job at the bakery, she decided to take a little detour and drive past the Highland House to see what it was like. Sierra counted the blocks as she headed toward the Willamette River.

Eleven blocks down, she spotted the old manor, now changed by the brightly painted mural across the north wall. Tall cedars circled the front of the huge house, protecting it from the busy street. A dozen yelling kids ran after a soccer ball in the front yard, and on the wide porch two girls played jump rope. An oval sign at the front gate proclaimed, "The Highland House." Smaller letters underneath read, "A safe place for a fresh start."

Sierra pulled into an open parking spot alongside the house and noticed a third person on the porch, turning the jump rope. The director, perhaps. He leaned against one of the pillars, and Sierra could hear him counting in a deep, resonant voice as the young girl jumped.

*I wonder what they'll want the four of us to do to help out here? I could turn the jump rope and count like that guy is.*

*Or maybe they'll want us to help the kids with their home-
work. This will be a snap.*

Part of her wanted to hop out of her car, march in, and
volunteer to help right then, especially because it
appeared only the one adult was present with the dozen or
so kids. But it was Tuesday night, and she had a ton of
homework. Her mom would most likely have dinner on
the table, and her parents would be concerned if she
didn't arrive home at her usual time after work.

Taking one last look at the cheerful house, Sierra
whispered, "I'll be back!"

Then, by the side of the house, she noticed a long line
of homeless people waiting to get into the Highland
Kitchen, where they served soup each night at 6:30. A
raggedly dressed old man with a bedroll slung over his
shoulder shuffled past her, checking a can of soda resting
on the low cement wall. The can apparently was empty.
He stopped under the streetlight several yards from the
soup kitchen line, and a look of hopelessness crossed his
bearded face.

Sierra's heart went out to him. Before she thought
about what she was doing, she grabbed the bag of leftover
Mama Bear's cinnamon rolls from the seat next to her, got
out of the car, and called to the stranger: "Do you like cinnamon rolls?"

Startled by her question, he eyed the bag curiously.

"Made fresh today," she explained, holding out her
gift. "I thought you might like them."

Sierra had never offered food to a homeless person

before. In the past, the homeless had seemed far removed from her world. Tonight, she felt differently for some reason. She felt responsible to do what she could. The sweet stillness of the late spring evening, along with the anticipation of helping out at the Highland House, bolstered her courage. She felt safe because the guy on the porch wasn't far away. If she needed to cry out for help, he was there.

She couldn't figure out why she felt so exhilarated about offering food to a homeless person. Perhaps it reminded her of when she was in Great Britain and the way she and her friends had boldly told strangers about a relationship with Christ. Maybe it was the delicate coolness of the evening breeze that reminded her of the description in Genesis about God walking with Adam and Eve in the garden in the cool of the evening. Whatever it was, right now God felt close . . . touchable . . . involved in the ways of humankind.

The scruffy-looking man slowly reached for the bag. "Thanks," he mumbled, turning his back so the others in line down the street wouldn't see what she had given him.

"You're welcome," Sierra said. "God bless you."

He didn't answer but dug his dirty hand into the bag.

She turned and headed back to her car. Glancing at the porch, she noticed the girls had stopped jumping rope. The guy was standing in the shadows, apparently watching her. She felt good and unsettled at the same time: good because she had done something that felt so right in reaching out to someone in need, unsettled because she had done so little to really help him. Where would he sleep? What would he eat for breakfast?

Driving home, she thought of how she would be greeted by her wonderful family, a bountiful dinner, and a warm bed. None of those things was available to that man. A strength and determination began to grow inside Sierra.

*I want to do more. I want to learn to live boldly and bravely for You, Lord, to reach out and really make a difference in this world You made.*

Unfortunately, Sierra's parents had a different view of her experience.

# *chapter five*

"**I** REALIZE YOU FELT SAFE," HER FATHER SAID, passing a bowl of peas at the dinner table, "but that's a rough area of town, Sierra. You don't know what could have happened."

"Yeah," her eight-year-old brother, Dillon, said, "he could have had a knife."

"Yeah," six-year-old Gavin chimed in, "or a machine gun."

"He didn't have a machine gun," Sierra said, scooping some brown rice onto her plate.

"You don't know," Dillon said. "It could have been in his bedroll."

"Yeah," Gavin said, "or up his pant leg. You shouldn't talk to strangers, Sierra. Isn't that right, Mom?"

Sharon Jensen gave Gavin the kind of tender smile a mother reserves for her youngest of six children. Turning to Sierra, her youngest daughter, she issued the same smile, adding a tightening of the space between her eyebrows, which was a sign of worry. "We would feel better if you didn't approach someone like that again unless

another person is with you. We applaud your zeal, honey.
We always have. Now season it with some common sense,
and we'll all feel a lot better."

"I sent for them yesterday," Granna Mae suddenly
chirped from her end of the table.

Sierra dearly loved her grandmother, as all of them did.
Some days her mind was as clear as still water in a
reflecting pool. Other times, like now, she would speak
nonsense, and an invisible blanket of concern would fall
on the family. Sometimes they would try to enter Granna
Mae's world by responding to her random statements.
Other times they let them go.

Tonight no one seemed sure what to do. Their eyes
checked the other family members' faces for subtle
signals. Granna Mae looked coherent as could be. Sierra
wondered, as she had so many times, how a person's
mind could betray her and go AWOL like that.

Granna Mae looked at them, startled by the sudden
silence.

"I hear what you're saying, Mom." Sierra picked up the
dropped conversation. "But here we sit, with all this food
and in this great big house. A lot of people out there need
help. I don't want to pretend they're not there. And if I
can help, I want to help."

"We're all for that," Dad said sternly. "All we ask is that
you always have someone with you. Understand?"

Sierra nodded.

"Isn't that how Christ sent out the disciples? In twos?"
Sierra's mom said. "It's the wise thing to do, Sierra."

Sierra nodded again. "You're right. I agree. I'll do that."

"How did I get the signals so messed up?" Sierra wrote in her journal later that night. "Here I think I'm doing something wonderful, giving food to that guy, and yet I upset my parents. How can something be so right and so wrong at the same time? Is it that I'm too impulsive?"

She was about to launch into a new topic, exploring the crazy avenues of how she felt about her dream of seeing Paul again and how immature she felt at the same time for feeding her crush. Just then Tawni entered their bedroom and slung her purse over the back of the desk chair.

"Hi," Sierra said. "How was your day?"

"Terrible." Tawni kicked off her shoes and wiggled out of her panty hose. "The results from this last month came in today, and guess who scored the absolute lowest in sales."

"You?" Sierra ventured. "But I thought when you did that Valentine special, they said you were the top promoter or something." Sierra didn't know much about the ins and outs of Tawni's job at the fragrance counter at Nordstrom, and she had never tried that hard to understand what Tawni meant when she rattled off news of her day.

"That was back in February," Tawni stated with an edge to her voice. One false move, and Sierra knew the edge of that verbal blade could slice right through her. Fortunately, a letter waiting for Tawni on her bed caught her eye, and she shut Sierra out.

Sierra pretended to refocus on her journal, but she was really watching her depressed sister as she slit the envelope with her long thumb nail and began to read the letter. Sierra had noticed the letter earlier but hadn't checked to see whom it was from. Jeremy probably—although he usually called instead of sending letters.

Over the top of her journal, Sierra could see Tawni's sullen expression lifting. She flipped to the second page of the letter, and a definite smile began to tug the corners of her lips, which now moved silently as she scanned the lines.

Sierra noticed how thin her sister's lips were. Tawni was beautiful, no question there. People would often turn and stare at her. Sierra had grown accustomed to that occurrence as they grew up, realizing all along that she would forever be the tomboy, destined to go unnoticed in the shadow of Tawni's beauty.

However, Sierra knew one thing: She had perfect lips. And now she realized for the first time that Tawni did not. Sierra had her mother's lips. Perfectly proportioned on top and bottom. And when she drew them back in a smile, her teeth fit in a neat row, and a dimple appeared. It comforted Sierra to discover that she had better lips than Tawni.

"I can't believe this!" Tawni half shouted, shaking the letter in the air and looking wildly at Sierra. "This is perfect." She jumped from her bed and burst through the doorway into the hall. "Mom? Dad?" she called out, running barefooted down the stairs.

"What?" Sierra said to the empty air surrounding Tawni's bed. A slight scent of gardenias had followed Tawni out of the room. Now Sierra had a decision to make. Should she go galloping downstairs and find out what her sister was so excited about? Or should she wait until Tawni returned?

An old conflict surfaced for Sierra. She and Tawni were sisters, and Sierra considered them to be friends as well. But they weren't super close, which was why Tawni ran to talk to Mom and Dad about her good news rather than stay in their room and let Sierra be the first to know.

Tawni had once blamed their lack of sisterly bonding on her being adopted and therefore not as intricately connected to Sierra as she would have been if they were blood relatives. Sierra claimed it was their personality differences.

She chewed thoughtfully on the end of her pen and kicked at a pile of clean socks at the foot of her bed. Glancing at her journal, she reread her last line: "Is it that I'm too impulsive?"

"Okay," she muttered, "then I won't be impulsive and run downstairs. I'll wait here, and when she comes back, I'll be sweet and interested and let her tell me her big news."

Snapping shut her journal, Sierra decided to put away her clothes. She matched up her socks and put them in the dresser drawer; then she hung up a mound of clean clothes draped over the chair. She even sorted out the papers in her backpack. Still Tawni didn't make an appearance. It was after 10:00, and Sierra was too tired to wait any longer. She got ready for bed and tried to select the best of all the options she had been contemplating about the letter's contents while cleaning her side of the room. Her conclusion was that the letter was from Jeremy, and he was coming to visit after all. Tawni had run downstairs to tell Mom and Dad, and then, of course, she had immediately called Jeremy. That's where she was now, making plans with him on the phone.

As Sierra turned off the light and pulled the covers up to her chin, she began to sift through the possible things she could say when she saw Paul again. Because if Jeremy was coming, she would certainly see Paul.

## chapter six

IERRA OVERSLEPT THE NEXT MORNING AND HAD to scramble to get ready. Tawni was still asleep when Sierra galloped down the stairs and bounded into the kitchen.

"What was up with Tawni and that letter last night?" she asked her mom, who was unloading the dishwasher.

Mom checked the clock and, handing Sierra a box of cranberry juice and a granola bar, said, "You'd better eat breakfast on the run. We'll talk about the letter when you come home."

These kinds of mysteries drove Sierra crazy. Charging out the front door with her backpack slung over one arm and the granola bar already stuffed into her mouth, she tried to punch the straw into her box drink.

*Okay, let's see. Jeremy is coming, but they didn't want to give me the details this morning because . . .*

No conclusion came to her mind except there simply wasn't enough time for a conversation. Slipping her free hand into her backpack, Sierra fumbled for her keys and started up the old VW Rabbit she shared with her mom.

During the 18-minute drive to school, Sierra went over all the assignments she needed to get cranking on. It was going to be a full week. She slipped into the first open parking spot she came to and hurried to her locker. Randy was waiting there for her.

"How you doing? You want to go to Lotsa Tacos for lunch?" he asked.

"Sure. Did you talk to Tre yet?"

Randy looked at her as if he didn't understand the question.

"About the service project at Highland House."

Randy nodded and said, "No, but I called there last night and set everything up. We're going to have to go two times to finish our four hours."

"That's okay," Sierra said.

"Yes, that's what I thought. I'll tell Tre today."

"Guess what? I drove by there last night and—"

Before she could finish her sentence, the bell clanged loudly over their heads. Sierra winced at the sound and gave Randy a nod. "I'll tell you the rest at lunch."

He appeared at her locker right on time for lunch. The guy had an unmistakable charm about him. As he stood there with his crooked grin, he looked at Sierra as if she were the only girl in the whole world.

"What?" she said, brushing past him and spinning the combination on her locker.

"You ready?" he asked.

"Yes," she answered with an affirming slam of the locker door.

"By the way," he said, "do you mind driving?"

"Oh, so that's it," Sierra said. "You asked me to lunch because you wanted a chauffeur."

"That wasn't the only reason."

"I suppose you want me to buy lunch for you as well."

"No," Randy said, taking her by the elbow and directing her out the front doors. "I got paid yesterday, so I have money for once."

"Good," Sierra said.

They crossed the parking lot to Sierra's car, and she climbed into the driver's seat. Reaching over to unlock the passenger door for Randy, she said, "I was only teasing you. The pay-your-own-way system seems to work best for us."

"That's 'cause we're a team!" Randy said, thumping the dashboard with his fists. "Unstoppable."

Sierra smiled at his antics. "I'm happy to tell you that I put my whole paycheck in the bank last week. I'm saving every penny."

"What are you saving for?"

"You know, that's a good question," Sierra said, pulling out of the parking lot and heading for Lotsa Tacos, which was less than three blocks from the school. "I don't need anything. I think I'm doing this savings thing on instinct. We were always taught to save our money when we were little, but I don't know what I'm saving it for."

Sierra pulled into the drive-through at Lotsa Tacos. The Rabbit hit the curb hard, and Randy said, "I know what you can spend all that money on. New shocks."

"I'd rather buy a new car," Sierra said. "Did you know

that Tawni bought her own car? I might need to do the same if this one decides to go belly up."

Four cars were in line ahead of them, and all of them were loaded with students from their school.

"So, what do you think they're going to have us do? At the Highland House, I mean," Sierra asked.

"I don't know. Paint maybe. Isn't it an old building?"

Sierra pulled the car up to the speaker. "It doesn't look too bad from the outside. Do you know what you want?"

Randy leaned over and shouted out his order. Sierra added a soft taco and a milk and began to drive forward.

"A milk?" Randy questioned. "Nobody orders milk with a taco."

"I do," Sierra said, sorting through the change in the glove compartment. "Oops! I don't have enough money. Do you have an extra quarter?"

"Oh, so you're one of those, are you!" Randy teased. "You have all your money tied up in stocks and bonds and rely heavily on your innocent friends to bail you out when you need cash."

Sierra pulled up to the window. "It's only a quarter, Randy. You make it sound like a crime."

"The only crime here is that you're drinking milk with your taco."

"I happen to like milk."

"I do, too. With cereal, or cookies, or even a turkey sandwich. But not with tacos—never with tacos."

"Just a second," Sierra said to the cashier. Then turning to Randy, she asked, "Are you going to give me a quarter or not?"

"Put your money away. I have this covered."

"You don't have to pay for the whole thing, Randy. Just loan me a quarter."

"Excuse me," the cashier said. "Would you two love-birds mind paying first and then moving forward to continue your spat?"

"Lovebirds!?" Sierra and Randy said in unison. They looked at each other and burst out laughing. Sierra snatched the money from Randy's fist and paid the whole bill with it.

"Keep the change," she said and drove forward.

"Keep the change!?" Randy spouted. "You just gave him a dollar tip."

Before Sierra could explain her impulsive action, Randy hopped out of the car and dashed back to the pay-ment window. She watched in her rearview mirror as Randy nodded his apologies to the woman in the car now in front of the window. He then pointed over his shoulder toward Sierra and spoke with the cashier, using lots of hand gestures.

As the bag of tacos was handed to Sierra through her open window, Randy jumped back into the passenger's seat. He waved the dollar bill in his hand and said, "Got it! Ha!" He was smiling and didn't appear at all bothered by her rash actions.

Sierra handed him the bag of food and pulled into the street, heading back to school. "You know what, Randy? I think I'm dangerous."

"I could have told you that," Randy said.

She shook her head. "I don't know what my mind is doing lately. I'm being reckless and impulsive. That wasn't fair to give him your money. I'm sorry." She drove into the school parking lot and found a spot for the car.

"Whatever," Randy said. "That's you, Sierra. You're a free spirit, and free-spirited people do crazy things sometimes. There's nothing wrong with that. Why are you being so hard on yourself? It didn't bother me."

"But it did bother you. Why else would you have gone back for the money?"

"Because I'm a tightwad." Randy opened the bag, pulling out her taco. He presented her with the carton of milk on his open palm as if he were serving it on a silver tray. "Your taco and milk, Miss Jensen."

"I feel as if I'm changing, Randy," Sierra said.

"People do," he said.

Sierra unwrapped her taco and asked, "Do you ever feel as if you're not sure who you are?"

"Sure. Everybody does sometimes."

"I never have before."

"Ever?" Randy said after he had swallowed his first bite of burrito.

"I don't think so."

Randy shook his head and stuffed another bite in his mouth. "Don't take yourself so seriously. You can act as impulsively around me as you want. I'll still be your friend. I might be out a couple of bucks now and then, but I'll still be your friend."

Sierra smiled and took a sip of her milk.

"Are you sure you don't want to go to the game Friday night?" Randy said, changing the subject and wolfing down his last bite.

"Not particularly. Are you going?"

"I thought about it. It would be a lot more fun if you came with me—I mean, with us. A bunch of people are going. Come on, Sierra. I'll even pay if you don't want to deplete your Swiss account."

"You're too nice," she said, enjoying having a guy be so understanding of her mixed-up feelings and so eager to spend time with her. Basketball didn't particularly thrill her, especially because the tickets were so expensive. But it would be fun to go with Randy and see how things turned out between Amy and Drake.

"Well?" he prompted.

"Okay, I'll go. I have the money, so I'll even buy my own ticket."

"Cool."

Smiling, Sierra motioned to Randy that he had a shred of cheese caught at the corner of his mouth. Randy had to be the only guy at school who still said "Cool." "Cool" and "Whatever" were his favorite words. And he was so easy to be around. It occurred to Sierra that what Amy was mistaking for a crush was simply a great friendship between the two of them. Not every girl had a buddy who was so understanding. Amy certainly didn't. No wonder she couldn't see this as merely a friendship.

# chapter seven

ON THURSDAY AFTERNOON, SIERRA SAT ON THE edge of her bed watching her sister wedge another pair of shoes into her suitcase and scurry to the dresser to pack her jewelry.

"I still can't believe you're going to Southern California," Sierra said.

Tawni had been floating ever since the mysterious letter arrived on Tuesday. In a few short days, it seemed as if Tawni's life had changed completely. Tomorrow morning, she and Mom and Dad were flying to Los Angeles for the weekend. Tawni's best friend from high school, Jennifer, had moved there with her parents. The letter was Jennifer's invitation for Tawni to come live with them.

"You didn't borrow my pearl earrings, did you?" Tawni asked, going through the neatly organized jewelry in her top drawer.

"Like I would," Sierra said, rolling onto her stomach. "What if Mom and Dad don't agree to let you move down there? What if you can't transfer to a Nordstrom store in that area?"

"That's why we're going this weekend. To find out," Tawni said impatiently. "Now, where's my gold bracelet?"

"Didn't you already pack your jewelry last night?" Sierra asked.

Like a skittish rabbit, Tawni hurried back to the suitcase on her bed and checked the pouch in the back. "You're right. I must be losing my mind!"

"You are losing your mind," Sierra chimed in, "to suddenly decide to move to Los Angeles like this."

"It's not Los Angeles. Jennifer lives in Carlsbad. It's only half an hour north of San Diego. I already told you this. The airfare was cheaper into LAX, and Dad thought the drive down the coast would be fun."

"When will Mom and Dad meet Jeremy?" Sierra asked.

"Tomorrow night. We're having dinner with his parents. Did I tell you I called the agent this morning?"

"What agent?"

"The modeling agent your friend's aunt referred me to."

Sierra nearly tumbled off her bed. "Modeling agent! I thought you said you didn't want to model?"

"I've been thinking about it. If I actually do have a chance, I should at least try it, don't you think?" Tawni definitely had stars in her eyes now. "The money would be a whole lot better than what I'm making, and besides, it might be kind of fun."

"Fun? Haven't you ever read those interviews with models who starve themselves and work 14-hour days and say they feel as if people treat them like objects rather than humans beings? How can you think that would be fun?"

"I'm not going to Paris, or even New York. It's a small agency, and I'd agree to model only clothing, not swimsuits. Mom and Dad and I have already talked about it. They think I should follow my dream and see what happens."

Sierra repositioned herself cross-legged on her bed and folded her arms across her stomach. "Since when did this become your dream, Tawni? It's as if you've turned into a different person ever since Jennifer's letter."

Tawni stopped her frenzied sorting and packing for a moment and looked softly at Sierra. "Maybe I have. Maybe this is what I've been waiting for, a chance to be on my own, trying something new, and enjoying the most fantastic relationship I've ever had with a guy. Living so far away from Jeremy has been torture. Would you expect me to turn all this down? For what? So I can stay here, where I have no friends, no future, no life?"

Sierra had known Tawni would leave home someday, just as their two older brothers had. She just hadn't expected it to be like this.

Neither of them spoke for a full five minutes. Tawni carefully folded and refolded a black blazer and then leaned on the top of her suitcase to close it. She stepped back, an expression of satisfaction crossing her beautiful face.

"Tawni?" Sierra said, getting up and shuffling the 10 or so feet to where her sister stood. "I love you, and I'm going to miss you. I hope everything works out." Sierra offered a big hug, which Tawni received with surprise.

"Honestly, Sierra, we're only going for the weekend to check things out. I'm not moving yet."

Sierra wanted to push her sister onto the floor, mess up her hair, and tickle her until she laughed. However, that technique hadn't worked when they were kids, and Sierra felt certain it wouldn't work now either.

"Well, just know that I'm happy all this seems to be working out for you."

"Thanks," Tawni said, picking up from her nightstand the "To Do" list she had written neatly on a flowered tablet. "Oh, right," Tawni muttered to herself. "Wrap thank-you gift for Jennifer's parents."

As Tawni set to work with her gift wrapping, Sierra retreated to the bathroom down the hall. Closing the door and locking it, she took a long look at herself in the mirror.

"What if I were beautiful like Tawni?" Sierra whispered to her reflection. "Would I want to run off to become a model? Or is it Jeremy she's really chasing?" Sierra grabbed a handful of her wild, curly blond hair and pulled it back from her face. She turned to the left and studied her profile.

Facing the mirror again, she smiled and watched her slight dimples appear. Her clear blue-gray eyes stared back, scanning each feature. Nose, chin, eyebrows, cheeks. All normal, she decided. A few too many freckles across her nose, perhaps. But then, there were always her lips—her perfect lips. She made a kissy face in the mirror and wondered if she were a little old to be doing this kind of self-image seeking. Didn't most girls do this when they were 12?

At 12, Sierra had been too busy riding horses and writing songs to stop and look in the mirror. At 14, she was still turning cartwheels in the yard with her younger brothers and raising rabbits for her 4-H project.

Now at 16, for the first time, Sierra realized she was almost grownup. Her family's move from a small town in the northern California Sierra Nevada mountains to the city of Portland had a lot to do with that. Her trip to England had also matured her. At least while she was there, she fit right in with the older students.

Sierra knew she was about to be left in the wake of her 18-year-old sister's departure. And all Sierra could think was that she wanted to go back and live her ideal childhood over again. Who needed the pressure of striving to get straight A's? Or the loss of an older sister right when they were starting to almost get along? And who needed a phantom like Paul in her life anyway?

Sierra let out a huge sigh. She didn't really feel like crying, but it would be nice to somehow expend these overwhelming emotions. Another long stare in the mirror brought a reflection of Paul to her mind. It must have been the eyes. Paul's eyes were the same color as hers. At least that's what the flight attendant had said when he looked at both of them sitting together on their flight into Portland.

With a tug at the drawer, Sierra pulled out her toothbrush, loaded it with toothpaste, and went to work scrubbing her teeth with all the vigor her emotions brought out.

*I'll never see Paul now that Tawni is going to San Diego. Jeremy has no reason to come here, so I have no reason to think I'll ever see Paul again. He's probably forgotten all about me.*

The foaming toothpaste began to drip from the side of her mouth. Sierra made a funny face like a raging monster before spitting it out.

*Amy's right. He is a dream I've made up. I do think about him too much.*

She rinsed her mouth and took a close look at her gleaming smile.

*And I'm probably too young for him anyway. Too impulsive and—what was it I told Randy the other day?—oh, yeah, dangerous. I'm too dangerous for Paul.*

Sierra grimaced fiercely at her reflection in the mirror.

Unexpectedly, some of Paul's final words to her before they parted company in the airport baggage-claim area came back to her. "Don't ever change, Sierra."

Sierra stood before the bathroom mirror, gazing into her eyes, which had turned the shade of a silent winter morning. In that instant, she remembered everything about Paul. The way he smelled like Christmas in Pineville, his searching blue-gray eyes, his leather jacket and Indiana Jones–style hat. The way he first approached her and spoke to her so openly.

Then, as Sierra had done 100 times in the past few months, she closed her eyes and prayed for Paul.

# *chapter eight*

THE NEXT NIGHT, SIERRA SAT HOME ALONE, except for Granna Mae, who was asleep upstairs. Settling in the swing on the front porch, Sierra picked at a box of raisins and listened to the plump doves cooing from the roof of the house across the street. Low clouds hung over the city, sending down a fine, warm mist.

Sierra felt so alone.

Randy, Amy, and Drake were on their way to the Blazers game at this very moment. Sierra had had to turn down the event because that afternoon Mom and Dad had left with Tawni. Someone needed to stay home and keep an eye on Granna Mae. Sierra was the only one available.

Earlier that afternoon, Sierra's oldest brother, Cody, had picked up the boys to keep them for the weekend at their home in Washington State, an hour's drive away. Cody and his wife, Katrina, liked it when Gavin and Dillon came to their "ranch" and kept their son, Tyler, company. Three-year-old Tyler adored his young uncles.

Amy had called in a panic half an hour ago, asking

Sierra's advice on what to wear. As Amy began to describe the outfit she had on, she had hung up with a squeal before Sierra could make a suggestion. Drake had arrived early.

Sierra had then tried to convince Granna Mae that a jaunt around the block would do her good. Granna Mae had broken her foot, and when the cast was removed not long ago, the doctor had encouraged her to exercise moderately. But tonight Granna Mae was weary and declined the offer, preferring the company of the television in her bedroom. Sierra had sat with her awhile watching a game show.

Within the first five minutes of the program, Granna Mae had nodded off. So Sierra had pulled a blanket over her and switched off the noisy television. The silence woke Granna Mae, and she irritably asked Sierra to "turn my program back on."

Sierra had obliged her beloved grandmother and then tiptoed downstairs and out onto the porch, where she now sat in her bunny slippers with her raisins and thoughts of Paul.

*Father God, are You tired of my praying about this guy? I don't know what it is. I just want Paul to stay on track with You. When I met him, it seemed he was falling away. Please keep him close to Your heart. I know it's his choice to obey You or to go his own way, but I pray that You'll keep Your hand on him always.*

It was unusually quiet, a strange occurrence around this old house. She thought back on how much things had changed. Her two older brothers had each left home, and now, if Tawni left, Sierra would be the oldest child there. Already she was experiencing the disadvantages of being the oldest, "responsible" child. She had had to give up the basketball game to watch Granna Mae. In a small way, Sierra could understand why her sister was looking forward to being on her own, running her own schedule.

Sierra tapped the last raisin out of the box and scuffed in her bunny slippers back into the house, where she headed for her favorite room, the study. An entire wall was covered with built-in bookshelves that reached from the floor to the ceiling and were filled with old books Granna Mae had collected over the decades. Some of them were in her native tongue, Danish. Sierra flipped on the soft amber light by the overstuffed chair and glanced around the room. Dozens of books silently called out, inviting her to slip between their cozy covers and spend the evening with them.

In the back of her mind paraded the long list she had written in her notebook of all the studying she needed to do this weekend. Being a young woman of determination, Sierra shunned the beckoning books and turned on the computer at her father's desk. The familiar soft whirring sound of the "brain" coming to life put Sierra into a studious mood. The assignment before her called for a 10-page report. She mentally increased that to 15 pages since she was conscientiously collecting every extra-credit point possible.

For almost an hour, she typed away furiously. Distant

footsteps sounded on the wooden floor of the entryway. Sierra assumed Granna Mae had awakened and was coming downstairs for a snack. To Sierra's surprise, Wesley, her older brother, poked his head into the library.

"What are you doing here?" Sierra said.

Wes greeted her with a kiss on the top of her head. "I didn't want you to be stuck here alone all weekend." Wes attended the University of Oregon in Corvallis, about a two-hour drive south of Portland. She would never admit to having a favorite among her four brothers, but in a lot of ways she was closer to Wesley than to the others.

"Where's Granna Mae?" he asked.

"Sleeping, I think. She was nodding off about an hour ago. I haven't checked on her since." Sierra clicked a few keys on the computer and closed down her project.

"You finished?" Wes asked.

"No, but a person can spend only so much time expounding on 'the benefits of the Industrial Revolution' on a Friday night before complete depression sets in."

"Why aren't you out with your friends tonight?" Wes seemed to have figured out the answer before he even finished his sentence. "Hey, I'm here now. I'll keep an eye on Granna Mae. Why don't you go do something? It's not that late."

"My friends are at a Blazers game."

"Wealthy bunch you're hanging out with these days."

"Not really. They buy the cheap seats. What about you? No interesting women to keep you company on a Friday night?"

Wesley stood with one shoulder leaning against a bookcase, running his fingers through his wavy brown hair. A slight smile graced his five o'clock-shadowed jawline. He looked just like their dad, or at least how their dad must have looked in his younger days before the crown of his head went bald.

"Not this week," Wes said casually. Sierra knew Wes had been interested in someone last Thanksgiving, only the woman hadn't seemed to return the interest. He hadn't talked about anyone since then.

"You want to do something?" Wes asked.

"Like what?"

"Rent a movie or go out for coffee."

"Sure. Do you think we should leave Granna Mae?"

"You're right," Wes said. "I forgot we're the only ones home with her. I think this is the quietest it's ever been around here."

"Strange, isn't it?" Sierra said. "It was worse the weekend I was alone with her when she had her surgery. This house is kind of creepy when it's empty."

"Have you checked the refrigerator yet?" Wes asked. "Is there any food?"

"I found some raisins," Sierra said, knowing that her brother hated them. Raisins, prunes, figs—any wrinkly fruit, he automatically boycotted.

Wes made a face. "Let's check on Granna Mae. She might be awake and feel like running out with us for a pizza."

"I doubt it, Wes," Sierra said with a laugh. "She's a

grandma, not a college student."

"That's part of her problem," Wes said, leading the way upstairs. "Everyone treats her as if she can't do anything for herself. Granna Mae is one hearty woman. She climbed into the treehouse out back with me when I was 14. Remember that? We had a picnic, just the two of us."

"Still, Wes," Sierra said, lowering her voice. "That was what—almost eight or nine years ago. A lot has happened since then."

"People are only as old as they think they are," Wes said, tapping gently on Granna Mae's bedroom door before turning the knob to open it.

Granna Mae stood by the window in her flowered robe, looking out into the night. The television was turned off. Mellow jazz music floated softly from her radio.

"I told you she would be up," Wes said to Sierra. Then raising his voice, he said, "How's my favorite lady?"

Granna Mae turned, startled to see them. Her eyes seemed preoccupied as they looked past Sierra and Wesley. Sierra involuntarily glanced over her shoulder to see if someone else stood behind her. Of course, no one was there. Granna Mae was experiencing one of her short-circuits of the brain.

"Yes?" she said cordially. She gave no indication that she had any idea who Sierra or Wesley was.

"I . . .," Wes began. "Or rather, *we* thought we'd check on you."

It seemed to Sierra he wasn't prepared for this disengaged greeting from his dear grandma. Then she realized that he wasn't home often. Sierra didn't know how many times he had seen Granna Mae like this.

"Yes," Granna Mae said evenly. "I'm fine."

"Would you like us to bring you anything?" Sierra asked.

"It appears my luggage hasn't arrived yet," she said. "If it wouldn't be too much trouble, could you check on it for me?"

Wes looked to Sierra. She gave him an affirming nod, and he said, "Sure. We can do that. Anything else?"

"No thank you." She shuffled across the room to where her purse sat on an old embroidered footstool. "I'll give you a nickel now and another if you return with my bags within the hour."

Wes looked pale.

Sierra spoke up. "That's awfully kind of you, but there's no need. Really. It's all complimentary."

"Oh." A pleased expression brushed over Granna Mae's face. "Well, thank you."

Sierra and Wes exited, closing the door behind them and making their way down the stairs in silence.

"Should we take some suitcases up there?" Wes asked.

"I don't think so. If we do, she'll only ask what they're for. She doesn't seem to stay on track with her scattered ideas. We should stay home for sure, though."

"I agree," Wes said. "Boy, that's sure strange, seeing her like that."

"I know."

They entered the kitchen, and Wes tapped the light

switch. The light turned on for a brief moment and then burned out.

"Whoa!" Wes said. "Where does Dad keep the light bulbs? Out in his workshop?"

"In the basement, I think," Sierra said. She kept in step with Wes as they searched for a light bulb and then returned to the kitchen and made quick work of replacing the burned-out one.

Out of habit, Sierra shook the old bulb and heard the slight rattling of the metal threads. Right before she tossed it into the trash, she thought of how frustrating it must be for Granna Mae to have a mind that didn't always make the connection, the way that burned-out bulb hadn't. For years and years, the switch automatically turns on and off at command. Then one day—poof! The switch is turned on as always, but the connection isn't made. Sierra shuddered to think of the day Granna Mae would be gone.

The feeling somehow applied to Tawni as well. Her whole life, Sierra had shared a room with her sister. It was entirely possible that would soon change.

When Wes wasn't looking, Sierra took the burned-out light bulb and tucked it in a drawer instead of pitching it into the trash. Later, when he wasn't around, she planned to take it up to her room.

# chapter nine

SIERRA WORKED AT MAMA BEAR'S BAKERY from 8:00 to 5:00 on Saturday. Amy came in during Sierra's lunch break, and they sat in the back room of the bakery eating broken bits of cinnamon rolls until they were sick of the gooey baked goods. Amy talked nonstop about the game and Drake. Apparently, he had done everything right: opened the door for her, bought her a Coke, paid attention to her all night, and walked her to the door—the perfect gentleman. Amy was glowing.

"I told Drake about our plan to fix dinner for him and Randy, and he thought it was a great idea!"

"Did you say anything to Randy?" Sierra asked.

"Of course. He was sitting right there."

"Amy!"

"What?"

Sierra knew it was best to go along with the whole scheme and not try to change Amy's big plans. "Nothing," she said, reaching for a napkin and wiping her sticky fingers. "Go ahead. What's our plan?"

"Okay." Amy's dark eyes lit up. "Next Saturday, my

house. We'll have lobster, baked potatoes, and . . . what else?"

"Salad of some sort?" Sierra suggested.

"Caesar," Amy decided. "And some kind of incredible dessert. Chocolate, of course."

"When are we going to make all this?" Sierra asked.

"We have to cook the lobsters fresh that night. I told you my uncle said he would give us four lobsters, didn't I? He doesn't usually serve them, but he can order them at a discount, so he's going to give them to us."

"That's nice of him."

"Maybe he can get us some chocolate cheesecake," Amy suggested. "I asked Drake, and he said he liked cheesecake."

"I have a feeling Drake will like anything we serve him," Sierra said. Then, because Amy looked at her strangely, she added, "And Randy, too. Have you ever met a guy who didn't like to eat?"

"I have a cousin who hates pasta," Amy said. "In our family, that's like saying, 'I hate to breathe air.'"

Sierra glanced at the clock above the sink and said, "I have to get back to work. Let me know if you want me to bring anything. And it's next Saturday, right?"

"Right. I told them 7:00. That will give us a little time to get everything ready."

"Sounds fun!" Sierra adjusted her apron as Amy exited through the back door. "See you," she called out and then returned to the front counter where Jody was the only one helping a long line of customers.

"You should have called me," Sierra said. "I didn't

realize it had gotten so busy."

"They all came at once," red-haired Jody answered. "One little cloud burst, and everyone wants coffee." She turned the knob on the espresso machine, and Sierra stepped to the register to ring up the order.

Sierra glanced up to see two more customers enter— Randy and Drake. She smiled at them and kept ringing up orders as Jody expertly made one cappuccino after another. When Randy and Drake reached the front of the line, Sierra noticed they both had wet hair.

"Did you stop to take a shower on your way in?" she asked.

"It was the other way around. A shower took us," Drake said.

"He was helping me with some of my Saturday regulars, and we had to stop right in the middle of one of the lawns, it was coming down so hard. I made the executive decision it was time for lunch." Randy's crooked smile lit up his face. He had such a friendly way about him. Sierra realized she felt comfortable and at ease whenever Randy was around—sort of the way she felt the night before when Wes showed up to help her with Granna Mae.

"Randy tells me these are the best donuts in town," Drake said. He ran a hand over his dark hair, taming all the wayward strands into place.

"Actually, we serve only cinnamon rolls, no donuts. Mrs. Kraus is considering getting a frozen yogurt machine, though."

"Two cinnamon rolls, then," Drake said.

"With lots of frosting," Randy added. "You always have to remind Sierra about the extra frosting."

"Are these boys friends of yours?" Jody asked.

"This is Drake and Randy," Sierra said. "And, yes, under pressure, I will admit that I know them both."

"Nice to meet you," Jody said. "Do you want something to drink with your rolls?"

"I'll have a mocha latte," Drake said.

Randy ordered two milks, and Sierra quickly said, "What you really need to go with those milks is a taco."

She was glad to see that Randy understood her teasing immediately and said, "No, no. Milk goes with cinnamon rolls, not tacos. This is what I've been trying to tell you."

"They have tacos here?" Drake asked.

"No," Sierra told him. "It's a little joke, that's all."

Drake glanced at Randy, who was still grinning, and then he looked back at Sierra. She realized that she had hinted at something she never had thought she would. Private jokes are common between boyfriends and girlfriends, and Drake seemed to be reading their expressions to see how close the two of them actually were.

For some reason, that made Sierra feel uncomfortable. She scooped up their cinnamon rolls as the two of them pooled their cash.

"You see," she began to explain to Drake, "I like milk with tacos, and Randy thinks that's weird."

"I like milk with tacos," Drake said.

"See?" Sierra challenged Randy. Her silver bracelets

clanged against the side of the cash register as she rang up
their order.

"So, is that what we're having at Amy's next week?"
Drake asked. "Tacos and milk?"

"No. Actually, she was just here. She'll be sorry she
missed you. Didn't she tell you what we're having?" Sierra
asked.

The guys shook their heads and reached for their rolls
and drinks.

"Then I won't tell either," Sierra said. "It'll be a
surprise."

Drake and Randy stepped to the side, making room for
the next customer as they chomped into their rolls.

After Sierra had helped the last two people in line,
Randy stepped back up to the register and said, "We think
what you and Amy are doing is really cool."

"You haven't tried our cooking yet," Sierra warned.
"You might want to reserve your opinion until after
you've lived through the experience."

"I'm willing to risk it," Drake said, looking at her with
an extra-warm smile that made her feel funny. He was
such a contrast to Randy—taller, with striking dark fea-
tures, broad shoulders, and that firm jaw, which he was
now sticking out as he smiled.

*If Amy were here,* Sierra thought, *she would think Drake
was flirting with me.*

But Sierra knew that Amy had little to worry about.
Flirting back had never been at the top of Sierra's skills.

## chapter ten

N SUNDAY EVENING, A LITTLE AFTER 8:00, Granna Mae and Sierra were sitting on the porch swing. That day Granna Mae had been lucid. Wes and Sierra had gone to church with her and to lunch afterward at her favorite restaurant. She had taken a nap in the afternoon while Sierra finished her paper and Wes took their St. Bernard, Brutus, for a run. Sierra had fixed grilled cheese sandwiches for supper, and Granna Mae had eaten hers with one dill pickle and a cup of strong black coffee, sipped from her favorite china cup.

All was normal. Sierra and Granna Mae had gone for a stroll around the block and now sat on the porch, chatting about birds. Cody and Katrina had dropped off Sierra's little brothers that afternoon, and Gavin and Dillon were on the front lawn wrestling with Wes and Brutus.

The peaceful May evening had just pulled down its shades, welcoming the night sounds and deep shadowed hues, when Dad pulled up in the van. He honked and called out the window his trademark "We're homely-home-home."

The boys ran to greet Mom, Dad, and Tawni. In a few minutes, everyone was gathered on the front porch asking questions over Brutus's incessant barking.

"Well?" Wes said. "How did it go? What did you decide?"

"Are you going to be a famous model?" Dillon asked.

"Did your luggage arrive okay?" Sierra asked.

"Do tell us, Nee Nee," Granna Mae said, using Tawni's childhood nickname, which Tawni couldn't stand.

Tawni looked at Mom and Dad. They both nodded their go-ahead. Facing the inquiring faces, Tawni announced excitedly, "I'm going! I'm moving to Carlsbad."

Even though this was the response they all had expected, a moment of silence hung over them as they each read the delight and eagerness written on Tawni's face.

"That's great!" Wes was the first to find his voice.

"Wow!" Sierra blurted out. "You're really going."

Tawni nodded and flashed an appreciative smile at Mom and Dad. "I wish you could have all met Jeremy's parents. They are such wonderful people."

"Yes, they certainly are," Mom agreed.

"Jeremy wasn't too bad either," Dad teased. "Tolerable. Not like that other guy in Pineville. What was his name? Marvin?"

"Martin!" Sierra, Wes, Tawni, and Mom all answered in unison.

"Right," Dad said with a twinkle in his eye. "The Martian boy."

"I hope he wasn't like this around Jeremy," Sierra said.

"No, thank goodness," Tawni responded.

Granna Mae tapped Sierra on the leg and said, "Now, who is Jeremy?"

Sierra leaned over and explained. "He's the guy Tawni met when she and I went down to Southern California for Easter vacation. He's friends with some of my friends from San Diego. Do you remember hearing about him? He is Paul's older brother."

A look of recognition came to Granna Mae's sweet, soft face. "Oh, yes. Paul. I do like that Paul. He brought me daffies, you know."

"Yes," Sierra said, "I remember. He visited you at the hospital."

"Yes, he did. I do like that Paul," Granna Mae repeated.

*So do I*, Sierra thought.

"We'd better carry the luggage inside," Dad said, turning to Wes, who was already following him to the van. "How was the weekend, son? We appreciate your coming up."

Sierra helped Granna Mae stand up as the women headed into the house. Everything felt so right to Sierra at this moment. She had Granna Mae's silky hand in hers, her little brothers were running into the backyard with hulking Brutus barking and following at a gallop. Everyone in her family except Cody, Katrina, and Tyler was there, within her view. She loved the scent in the air after the rain, the excited tone in Tawni's voice, the warm feeling that washed over her when Granna Mae said Paul's name.

Sierra wanted everything to freeze right there, even the moths on the screen door. This was her home, her family, her life. She didn't want it to change. Truth be told, she didn't want Tawni to leave.

How could she possibly feel this way? And since she did, how could she tell her sister?

An hour later, the two of them were alone in their room. Tawni bubbled over with details as she unpacked. Wearing her favorite pj's, Sierra was curled up in bed taking in every word.

Tawni seemed to have come alive since this adventure began. She was excited about everything. Already she had told Sierra about their meeting with the modeling agent on Saturday and how the agent had said he thought Tawni had a good chance of finding work right away. She also had explained to Sierra how ecstatic Jennifer was about Tawni coming to live with them. Now she was recounting that she would request a transfer to a Southern California Nordstrom on Monday and move down as soon as she could. Everything seemed perfect.

Except for the pierced feeling in the center of Sierra's heart. She wanted to protest, "You can't leave. Not yet." She never had expected she would feel this way.

"I'm glad for you, Tawni. I really am. I just can't believe you're going," Sierra said, taking a deep breath. "Actually, I wish you weren't going. I'm going to miss you something fierce!"

In one fluid motion, Tawni swished across the room and flung her arms around Sierra's neck. She gave Sierra a light hug and graced her cheek with a kiss.

"Think of it this way: You'll have the whole room to yourself." Tawni's smile remained in place as she fluttered back to the nearly empty suitcase.

*How can she be so casual about this?* Sierra thought. *I'm opening myself up to her for one of the first times ever, and she's being sweet and kissing me. Why wasn't it like this before? Will it ever be like this for us again?*

# chapter eleven

S IERRA HAD LITTLE TIME TO CONTEMPLATE HER relationship with her sister during the next week. On Monday, in Mr. Rykert's class, they spent the period in their teams discussing their outreach projects. Randy had some notes on what they were supposed to do and started to suggest who should do what.

Vicki pulled a ponytail holder from her wrist and twisted her hair into it. "Will you guys excuse me a minute? I'll be right back." She went over to the corner where Amy and Byron were sitting and started to talk to them. Amy and Vicki had been close friends when Sierra started attending this school in the middle of the year. Then Vicki began to date a senior, and Amy seemed ready for a new friend. That's when she and Sierra started to do things together.

"We're scheduled to go to the Highland House Tuesday and Friday," Randy said. "The director asked if we could tell a Bible story and maybe sing a song with the kids. Then we'll spend the rest of the time helping them with homework and playing with them."

Tre looked indifferent. Sierra couldn't tell if he was

with them or not.

"You want to organize the story?" Randy asked, looking at Sierra.

"Sure. Sounds easy enough."

By the next afternoon, when the four of them stood inside the meeting room at the Highland House, Sierra discovered she had spoken too soon. Telling a story to this bunch of kids was not easy. To even sit on the floor and listen was more than most of them could handle after being in school all day.

Sierra had worked until almost midnight cutting out, pasting, and coloring Bible characters that she had fastened to pencils so she could hold them up as puppets while she told the story of the prodigal son. She had enough puppets so that Randy, Vicki, and Tre could all help her hold them up as she did the storytelling.

Tre didn't understand what she wanted him to do, so he retreated to a far corner of the large room to watch. Vicki didn't get into the spirit of the activity and spent all her time telling the children to hush.

But Randy jumped in enthusiastically, especially when it was his turn to hold up the pigs from the pigpen where the prodigal had his change of heart. Randy had those pig puppets dancing and snorting and stealing the show. The kids laughed and started to imitate the pig noises.

"Randy," Sierra whispered, "the prodigal is supposed to realize he doesn't want to stay in there with the pigs!"

Randy kept the pigs dancing and leaned over to answer without taking his eyes off his captive audience. "Hey, at least they're listening. Come on, hit 'em with the moral of the story while we have their attention."

Sierra tried to conclude with the point that the young man returned home and his father was watching and waiting for him. Only, Vicki had the father puppet, and she held it out in front of her like a lit sparkler she was afraid would get sparks on her.

"And God is just like that," Sierra concluded, feeling frustrated with Vicki that she wasn't making the father-God figure a little more appealing. "He loves us and wants us to come to Him. He wants us to say we're sorry for all the wrong things we've done, and He wants us to turn our lives over to Him."

The puppets were then put to the side, and Sierra was the only one standing before the kids. She was losing their attention fast.

"If any of you would like to do that," she said, feeling herself stumbling over the words, "if you'd like to pray and give your life over to God, then we'd like to talk to you afterward."

Several kids were meandering to the back of the room, anticipating the opening of the double doors so they could be released to play.

"Before you go," Sierra said, her voice rising and carrying a bit of a desperate edge to it, "I'd like to pray with you guys. Everyone please stop where you are and close your eyes."

She waited a moment, looking around the room. Only two little girls in the front closed their eyes, and one of them started to peek.

"Come on, you guys," Randy said loudly, stepping next to Sierra. "Stop where you are and close your eyes."

Now they were all looking at Randy, including the two girls who had previously had their eyes closed.

"Better go ahead and pray," Randy muttered to Sierra.

Sierra closed her eyes and bowed her head, knowing she was probably the only one in the room doing so. Her prayer was four short lines and her "Amen" came out faster than even she imagined it would.

"Okay!" Randy called over the kids' rumbling. "You're dismissed." He didn't need to say it twice.

Tre, Vicki, and Randy followed the herd of noisy kids out the doors, leaving Sierra to pick up.

*Well, that was a bomb,* Sierra thought in disgust. *And look at this floor! How could these kids have made such a mess in so short a time?*

Smashed paper cups, left over from snack time, were everywhere. Some had been shredded into tiny bits and sprinkled across the floor like confetti. Muttering to herself, Sierra grabbed a trashcan and began cleaning up the cups.

*They didn't hear a word I said. What a disaster!*

"Prodigals seem to be your specialty," a male voice behind her said.

"Hardly," Sierra said dryly, without looking up.

"Why? You think they don't ever change, Sierra?"

It was his voice, saying her name. Holding her breath, Sierra turned and looked into the face she had carried around in her memory for months. Paul's.

## *chapter twelve*

S IERRA FELT THE BLOOD RUSHING TO HER cheeks and found her voice had taken a sudden vacation without telling her.

Paul stood only a few feet away, looking casual and unruffled. His thick, wavy brown hair fell across his broad forehead, giving him the look of a windblown adventurer. He was clean shaven, and a hint of sunburn flashed across his cheeks and his thin, straight nose. Or was it possible that Paul was blushing as well?

He held the prodigal puppet in his hand and twirled the pencil between his fingers, spinning it back and forth. He didn't speak but gazed at her through clear blue-gray eyes that smiled at her even though his lips remained still.

"Hi," Sierra managed to squeak out. She brushed her hair from her face and tried to take a deep breath. Her heart pounded wildly, and she felt her lips quiver as she tried to form a smile.

"Hi," Paul said calmly. "What happened to your boots?"

"You mean my dad's old cowboy boots?"

He nodded.

"The sole came off the right boot. I haven't taken them in to be fixed yet." *He remembers what I was wearing when we first met.*

"I never had a chance to thank you for the flowers you took to Granna Mae in the hospital. She really appreciated them."

"How's she doing?"

"Good. Great, really. She's doing fine." *Stop yourself, Sierra. You sound like a parrot!*

The room grew silent. Sierra and Paul held each other's gaze for a long, uninterrupted moment. For some reason, Sierra felt herself calming down and drawing closer to Paul even though she hadn't moved an inch.

"I want to tell . . . ," Sierra began.

"There's something I . . . ," Paul said at the same instant.

They both released a nervous laugh, followed by a "You first," which also came out in unison.

"Go ahead," Paul said. This time he was smiling at her, not only with his eyes, but also with his lips.

"I, um . . . well . . ." Sierra couldn't get her thoughts and her words to cooperate. Part of her wanted to run into Paul's arms and say, "I've been praying my little heart out for you, and here you are at a Christian outreach mission. Does this mean my prayers have been answered? Are you done with walking away from the Lord?"

Another part of her was still in shock at suddenly seeing him. That part of her wanted to turn and run like the wind.

Suddenly, the double doors burst open, and two little girls with small braids all over their heads called out, "There you are, Paul. Come turn the jump rope for us."

Paul didn't answer them but kept staring at Sierra.

"Come on," they cried, running over and grabbing his arms.

Paul reached over and gently tapped Sierra on the forearm with the first two fingers on his right hand. "We need to talk sometime," he said in a low voice.

The persistent girls pulled at him, and he added, "By the way, Clint really appreciated the rolls."

"Clint?"

"Last week," Paul said as the girls urged him to come with them. "I saw you on the sidewalk out front. I saw you give Clint the bag, which he told me was filled with cinnamon rolls."

"That was you on the porch?" Sierra asked.

Paul nodded and allowed himself to be dragged from the room. As he passed Sierra, a fresh-from-the-forest scent touched her nose.

"Whose turn is it to jump first today?" he asked, wrapping an arm around each of the girls.

The doors closed behind them, and Sierra lowered herself to the floor with a plop. There she sat, stunned, trying to absorb what had just happened. She knew her friend Katie would call this a "God-thing," this coincidence that Paul just happened to be at the same place where she was assigned to do her service project. But why? What was he doing there? Obviously, the kids knew him, so he had been coming for a while. Did he work there for pay? Was he a volunteer? Why would he volunteer to help? This was the last activity she would have pictured him doing based on her first impression of him. But he seemed changed.

"Hey, Sierra!" a male voice called out, and the double doors swung open.

Sierra looked up expectantly.

It was Randy. "Are you coming out here? I could use some help at my homework table."

"I was just, um, cleaning up here a bit. I'll be right there." She wondered if her face still looked as red as it felt.

"Cool," Randy said, exiting with a single wave of his hand. Sierra quickly scooped up the final pieces of trash and stuffed the puppets into her backpack. When she picked up the prodigal, Sierra spun the pencil slowly between her fingers the way Paul had. What had he meant about her specialty being prodigals? Did he see himself as a prodigal who had come back?

When they had met, he had told her about his girlfriend, and Sierra had lectured him on the folly of dating someone who wasn't a believer. Paul's reaction had been to pull back from Sierra, and that was that. Or was it? Had her months of prayers for him had an effect?

Her heart was still pounding fast when Sierra emerged from the meeting room and found her way into the former dining room of the old mansion. Several tables were set up around the room, where the children could do their homework. Randy seemed to be the only person available to help the 15 or so kids. Paul wasn't there. Maybe it had only been a dream. The lack of sleep last night, the stress of the rowdy kids . . . maybe she had only imagined that Paul had stood beside her, that he had looked at her and smiled, that he had reached over and touched her arm with his fingers. She touched the spot where Paul had tapped her arm, as if it might help her sort her dreams from reality.

"Over there," Randy said, pointing to a round table where five kids sat with the same worksheet in front of them. "They're doing fractions. Can you help them?"

Still lost in her cloud, Sierra made her way to the table and sat down in a small chair. The little boy next to her smelled awful. The odor hit her like smelling salts, reviving her from her dream. She could hardly stand to be near him. The odor was so strong Sierra casually covered her nose with her hand. She remembered reading a book about a young schoolteacher in the Appalachians who had to carry a hanky laced with perfume because her students smelled so bad. Throughout the day, the teacher would hold it to her face, filtering out their terrible odor.

"Okay. You're done," Sierra said as soon the boy finished. "You can go outside and play now."

He pushed back his chair, looking eager to leave. But instead of walking away from the table, he came over to Sierra and looked into her face. "Are you going to come back tomorrow?" he asked, his brown eyes pleading.

"Ah, no," Sierra said, trying to hold her breath and speak at the same time.

He looked disappointed, but he wasn't moving.

"I will be back on Friday," she added quickly.

His expression lit up. "I'm Monte," he said. "You remember me, okay?"

"Okay," she agreed. "I'll remember you." *Believe me, Monte, I'll remember you, all right.*

He left, and Sierra let out her breath, ready for some fresh air.

"Will you do art with us on Friday?" one of the girls asked. "We don't have to do homework on Fridays, but we can do art if someone helps us."

"Sure," Sierra agreed. "I'll do art with you on Friday."

"Every Friday?" another girl asked.

"Well, at least this Friday," Sierra said. She now understood why the director had been so thrilled when their foursome showed up that afternoon. He said they were short-staffed. Sierra could see how desperately the kids wanted someone to pay attention to them.

The other children at her table finished, and they all wanted to go outside to play soccer with Sierra.

She let them lead her by the hands. When they went out front into the big yard, Sierra immediately spotted Paul. He wasn't playing jump rope. Tre had taken that position. The two little girls were turning the rope, and Tre was the one jumping. It was the first time Sierra had seen him smile or heard him laugh. Those little girls had accomplished what none of the teens at Sierra's school had been able to do. The girls had made friends with Tre.

Paul stood in the center of the yard with a whistle

around his neck and a soccer ball under his arm. He was calling out directions when Sierra was hauled into the mob by her new fan club.

"She's on our team!" they yelled.

Paul looked at her with what Sierra interpreted to be a mix of admiration and surprise.

"Okay, then," he called out, tossing the ball into the air. "It's every kid for himself. The goal is the oak tree."

He blew the whistle and immediately the 20 or so grade-school kids began to clamor for the ball.

"This way," the girls squealed, dashing after the ball.

Sierra jogged along with them, noticing that Randy had set himself up as the goalie. With a quick glance over her shoulder at Paul, Sierra knew once and for all that he wasn't a dream. He really was standing there, wearing that smile—the one that started in his eyes and lit up his face. And he was staring right at her.

The soccer-playing little girls huddled close to Sierra as they charged toward the oak tree. It was a warm afternoon, and Sierra wished she had worn shorts instead of jeans. The lively gang of soccer players ran all over the yard, and Sierra trotted along with them until finally one of them hit the ball past Randy and made a goal by slamming it against the oak tree.

That kid then replaced Randy as the goalie, and the game continued. Only now Randy was jogging alongside Sierra, giving her advice as they went.

"Kick it out toward the front fence," Randy said. "I'll be waiting for it."

He started to run off as Sierra was saying, "But Randy, this is for the kids!"

Suddenly, the ball was before her, and without hesitation, she kicked it toward the front fence. Randy was ready as promised, and he slammed it into the tree before the goalie even had a chance to turn around.

"Yahoo!" Randy shouted, arms in the air. "Way to go!"

He ran over to Sierra and gave her a high five with both hands, leaning close to say in her ear, "I told you we make a great team!" Spontaneously, he wrapped his arms around her in a quick hug.

Sierra felt prickly from her neck up. Randy's gesture was the most affectionate thing he had ever done. She knew Paul had observed it all. The blush crawled from her neck up to her cheeks and then burst like a sunrise across her sweaty forehead.

"No fair!" the kids began to yell. "You two can't do that."

"You know what," Sierra said, wiping the perspiration from her top lip as she saw Paul coming closer. "I think I'll step out this next round."

"Not now," Randy said. "With a little strategy, we can have this thing wired."

"Don't leave!" Sierra's little fan club cried, grabbing her arms.

"Come on," one of the older boys called out. "Throw the ball in, Paul. Let's play."

"Everyone ready?" Paul asked. He now stood less than six feet away, the group of eager players huddled around him. Sierra could smell Monte again, only she wasn't sure if her own armpits were contributing to the sudden air pollution as well.

"I'm out for this round," Sierra said to the little girls beside her. "I need to check on something inside." She hurried away before anyone could see how red her face was.

She didn't look back, so she would never know what Paul's face looked like as he watched her go.

# chapter thirteen

"⟪T⟫HAT'S WHAT I'M SAYING," SIERRA STATED emphatically on the phone with Amy later that evening. She had repeated the whole scenario to Amy and concluded with, "The worst part is, nothing happened. Paul left before I did, and now I don't know if he'll be there Friday or not."

"So, you're telling me that for one brief moment you two spoke, and now Paul is back to being a phantom."

"In a way, yes. But don't you think it's a God-thing?"

"Well," Amy said, "I hate to be the realist here, but nothing happened, Sierra. I mean, he was there, but all he did was look at you, say a few words, and disappear."

"I know, but when he looked at me, it was as if the rest of the room started to fade away into smeared watercolors."

"Oh, please!" Amy started to laugh. "You are so melo-dramatic, Sierra. Nobody really feels like that when she's around a guy."

"I'm not making this up, Amy. That's exactly how I felt."

"So, where was Vicki the whole time?" Amy asked.

"She was playing jacks with a little girl on the back porch."

"She didn't see Paul, then?"

"I don't know. Why?"

"I was curious, that's all. If Vicki noticed Paul, I'm sure I'll hear about it."

There was a stretch of silence as Sierra tried to keep her imagination from spinning out of control. Vicki had a tendency to attract and hold the attention of most of the guys she set her sights on. Would Paul be the next one on her list?

"Why don't you come with us to the Highland House this Friday?" Sierra wasn't sure what this would prove, but it seemed like a good idea as she said it.

"I can't. That's when Byron and I are doing our service project. Oh, did I tell you that next weekend I'm going to start working at my uncle's restaurant?"

"Did another hostess quit?" Sierra was finding it difficult to be thrilled about Amy's news when her own news about Paul was still on the conversation table, even if Amy wasn't devouring it the way Sierra had. Amy wasn't even sampling it.

"Yes. He wanted me to start this Saturday, but I told him I already had a commitment. When do you get off work on Saturday?"

"Probably 4:00."

"Why don't you come straight to my house, and we'll start dinner for Randy and Drake. Did I tell you I got a chocolate cheesecake for us?"

Sierra had forgotten about the dinner. "Great."

"Oh, well, you sound excited. Don't you like cheese-cake?"

"No. I mean yes. I like cheesecake."

"Okay. Good. I better get going," Amy said. "I'll see you at school tomorrow. Wait for me by my locker in the morning, okay?"

Sierra waited until the bell rang, but Amy never showed up at her locker the next morning. Slipping into class right before the tardy bell, Sierra pulled out her assignment to hand in. She had been up late again, trying to type her report in spite of the way her mind kept wandering to Paul. What had he thought of her? Why didn't he say anything more to her? Would she see him again?

So much had been going on at her house last night with all of Tawni's plans that Sierra hadn't tried to redirect the conversation to herself and Paul. When Amy had down-played the encounter, Sierra decided not to make a big deal out of it with anyone else.

The funny thing was, she wanted to tell Randy. He was her buddy. She told him lots of things, including how she felt about Tawni leaving. And Randy was there at the Highland House. He had met Paul. Certainly, Randy of all people would agree with her that it was a God-thing.

Somehow she couldn't bring herself to tell him. She was still trying to convince herself that his brief hug at the soccer game was only a brotherly expression of joy over their victory. Still, it had confused her. Funny thing—she hadn't even thought to tell Amy about the hug. Amy would have loved to hear all about that since it came from Randy. Sierra decided she wouldn't tell Randy about Paul and she wouldn't tell Amy about Randy's hug. It wasn't important.

Then, on their way to the cafeteria for lunch, Amy complicated things. She told Sierra she had been talking to Vicki in the parking lot and that's why she hadn't made it to her locker that morning.

"I asked Vicki if she had met a guy named Paul, and she said she saw some guy out in the yard playing soccer with the kids, but she didn't know his name."

"You didn't tell her I knew him, did you?"

"Well . . ." Amy lowered her big brown eyes.

"You did. What did you tell her?"

"Oh, not much."

"You told her everything, didn't you?"

"Vicki and I have been friends a long time," Amy said, quickly defending herself. "She won't say anything to anyone. I told her not to."

"Amy, that really ticks me off!" Sierra turned to her friend and embarked on the first argument of their friendship.

"Sor-ry!" Amy retorted in an exaggerated tone.

"You knew I was telling you all those things about Paul in confidence," Sierra said, stopping in front of the cafeteria door and stepping to the side. "I feel betrayed. You didn't have my permission to share those things."

Students streamed past them. Sierra spoke only loud

enough for Amy to hear her. Amy looked away as if she were a little kid who had just gotten in trouble.

Feeling her temper cool, Sierra said, "I wish you hadn't been so free with my personal life, Amy, that's all. Back at Easter when you found out I thought Randy had invited me to that formal dinner when really he had been asked by Vicki, you told me you were good at keeping secrets."

"I said that?"

The blood began to drain from Sierra's face. "You didn't say anything to Randy, did you?"

Amy's face gave away the answer. "I only told him because he was trying to figure out how you felt about him," Amy said.

"He could ask me that!" Sierra spouted. "Any time! Any day! He knows I'd tell him the truth." She caught her breath in the now empty hallway and said, "Is that why you've been pushing for me to spend time with him? Because you told him I liked him, and now you're trying to verify your statement?"

"You make it sound so cold and cruel," Amy said.

"I think it was inconsiderate," Sierra shot back. "You were talking behind my back about my personal feelings and about information I had shared with you in confidence."

Sierra felt as if she were in junior high all over again, squabbling with her best friend. The image calmed her down. Maybe in a way she was still on a junior high level when it came to dating. She wasn't experienced like Vicki or eager like Amy. Instead, she was absorbed by this all-consuming crush on an older guy.

"You're right," Amy said, looking soberly at Sierra. "I said too much to Vicki and to Randy. I am sorry, really. I apologize."

Sierra let out a huge breath and said, "Apology accepted. Come on. Let's get some lunch." One thing Sierra did well was fight fair. She had learned early in her family to express herself openly and accurately. She also had learned the most powerful position in an argument was to be the first one to forgive and forget.

"You're not mad anymore?" Amy asked.

"I'll get over it. I told you I accept your apology, and I do. I won't hold it against you anymore."

"Wow," Amy said as they headed for their usual table.

"Wow?"

"That was the quickest I've ever been pardoned. In my family, you have to wash someone's car or make his favorite cake before he'll even begin to think about forgiving you."

Sierra smiled. It certainly wasn't that way in her family.

"Can we join you guys?" Sierra asked as they stopped at a table in front of Drake, Randy, and four other people. Vicki wasn't in the bunch, which made Sierra feel better, knowing that the topic of Paul was less likely to come up.

"You're really different, Sierra," Amy said.

"Thanks. I think."

"How is she different?" Drake asked, lifting a nacho chip to his mouth and catching the dripping cheese before it globbed all over the cafeteria tray.

"Is that all they have today?" Amy asked, avoiding Drake's question. "Nachos?"

"There are sub sandwiches, too," Randy said. "Did Sierra tell you what a great time we had at the Highland House yesterday?"

"As a matter of fact, she did. I heard a lot of interesting individuals were there." Amy's slightly raised eyebrows hinted that she knew more than she was saying.

Sierra held her breath, waiting to see if Amy would say anything more about Paul.

"I'm going to buy a sandwich," Amy said, letting her previous comment drop. "Anyone else want anything?"

Sierra shot her friend an appreciative glance for keeping her comments to a minimum.

"Hey, I had an idea, Sierra," Randy said. "When we go back on Friday, why don't we go for a pizza afterward?"

"Do you mean all of us? Tre and Vicki, too? And maybe some of the staff at the Highland House, if they're available to join us?"

"Oh." Randy sounded surprised. "Sure. That'd be fine with me."

Sierra turned to Tre, who sat quietly on the other side of Drake, and said, "Would you like to go out for pizza with us on Friday after we're finished at the Highland House?"

Tre caught her eye and nodded. She was pretty sure he knew what she had just asked. At any rate, she had made the pizza event a safe situation. Regardless of what Amy may have said to Randy, now he couldn't read into their friendship any kind of message that Sierra was spending time with him because she wanted to be considered his girlfriend.

Digging her thumbnail into her orange, Sierra listened to the ruckus all around her in the small cafeteria and tried to figure out if she had truly calmed down after the confrontation with Amy.

*Is my heart right with You, Lord?* Sierra thought as she slipped the first orange wedge past her lips and let the sweet juice burst in her mouth. *I don't want to get things out of whack here.*

But she had the feeling it was too late. Her life felt as if it were about to spin off into outer space.

## chapter fourteen

*S*IERRA TOOK A LONG TIME TO DECIDE WHAT TO wear on Friday morning. She got up early to take her shower and to have ample opportunity to choose just the right outfit.

She was slipping into her third option when Tawni rolled over in bed and said, "What's with all the wardrobe changes?"

Since Sierra had time, she went over to Tawni's bed and gingerly sat on the edge. Talking like this with her sister was a new experience, and she approached it cautiously. She had so much stored inside her, things she hadn't said to Amy since the confrontation outside the cafeteria, things she couldn't tell Randy.

"I might see Paul today."

Tawni propped herself on her elbow and looked interested. "Oh?"

With this hint of encouragement, Sierra decided to tell Tawni everything. "Did Mom say anything to you about what happened at the Highland House last Tuesday?"

"No. You know Mom. She wouldn't say anything

unless you told her to tell me. With Mom, mum's the word!" Tawni chuckled at her own little joke.

Sierra thought it was kind of irritating the way Tawni was so perky and happy lately, even first thing in the morning, which used to be her worst time of day.

Sierra explained a little about Randy being on her ministry team. And then she plunged in and told Tawni about Paul coming into the room on Tuesday and saying what he did about prodigals and then leaving at the end of the day without talking to her again.

Tawni looked interested as the story continued.

"But now I might see him today, and I'm kind of nervous," Sierra confessed. "Actually, I'm terrified. I've never gone through this before."

"First thing you do," Tawni said, now fully awake, "is to pray. Always pray."

Sierra almost laughed. "That's what I've been doing. For months, I've been praying for Paul. Not that I would see him again. I've been praying that he would get really close to the Lord."

"You have?" Tawni's expression took on a hint of awe. "I'd say God is answering your prayers then, because Paul is going to Scotland this summer to work at a mission their grandfather started."

"He is?" Sierra's heart sank. "When is he leaving?"

"I'm not sure. Pretty soon." Tawni snapped her fingers. "You know what else I just figured out? The Highland House is connected with the one their grand-father started in Scotland. I remember Jeremy asking me if I'd heard of it because his uncle runs the one here in Portland. I think Paul is staying at the Highland House since his school is already out, and he didn't have the money to go home to San Diego and then fly to London."

Tawni's words, "fly to London," brought back all kinds of memories. Sierra wished she were going on another flight to London—the same flight as Paul.

"You know what we should do," Tawni said. "I'll ask Mom if we can invite Paul and his uncle to come for dinner one night before I leave for San Diego and Paul leaves for Scotland."

Sierra liked the idea immediately.

But before Sierra's imagination could spin a web of dreams, Tawni said, "Try to remember, Sierra, if it's meant to be, it's meant to be. If it's not, it's not."

For Tawni, that was a deep thought, and Sierra knew she was right. Even so, the many connections between Sierra's family and Paul's were intriguing as well as encouraging.

"Sierra," Mom called through the closed door, tapping it lightly with her fingers before opening it, "I need to keep the car today, so I'll drive you to school. Will you be ready in about 10 minutes?"

"Yikes!" Sierra glanced at the clock on Tawni's dresser and sprang into action, pulling the rest of her outfit together. She settled on the basics: jeans, a white T-shirt with a cotton woven vest, and a collection of leather and bead braided bracelets on her wrist with matching bead earrings.

Sierra made it to school on time but found it nearly impossible to concentrate on any of her classes. So many feelings were colliding inside of her: eagerness to see Paul again, the possibility of his coming for dinner, and if she saw him today, the variety of things she could say to him. She had practiced several conversations in her head the night before while she was trying to fall asleep. One of the conversations involved Sierra being honest with Paul and not joking around or teasing the way she usually did when she talked to guys. She told Paul how much she had prayed for him over the months. In her half-awake, half-asleep state, she imagined Paul had taken her hand in his and held it tightly.

Sierra shook away the memory of her dream. She needed to catch the teacher's final homework instructions. It was time to put her thoughts of Paul into the invisible treasure chest in her heart and lock them up until at least the afternoon.

Randy met Sierra at her locker at lunch and told her that he and Tre were going to eat outside since the weather was so nice. Randy said he could use her help in preparing the story for that afternoon. Since Sierra had done all the work last time, Randy and Vicki were supposed to do the story this time.

Sierra joined Randy and Tre, feeling a little bit as if she were hiding from Amy. Her mind was so full of Paul that Sierra didn't trust herself not to say anything to Amy.

"Where's Vicki?" Sierra asked.

"She has other plans, I guess," Randy said, pulling out

his guitar and tuning it up. He didn't seem bothered by her lack of assistance. "She said she would meet us there this afternoon."

As Randy strummed his guitar, he softly sang the three songs he planned to teach the kids. Tre seemed to watch Randy's every move on the guitar. "Do you want to try it?" Randy said, offering the guitar to him.

Randy's gesture touched Sierra. She pretty much ignored Tre, but Randy treated him like a friend, even turning over his guitar to him. Sierra knew how highly Randy valued his guitar. He had brought it to Sierra's house one time and had played a song he wrote, but he didn't let Gavin or Dillon play it.

Tre shyly reached for the instrument and began to strum. To Sierra's and Randy's amazement, he started to sing old American pop tunes, accompanying himself on the guitar without flaw.

"When did you learn to play like that?" Randy asked. "You're very good!"

"My brother plays guitar," Tre said. "He taught me."

Sierra was certain it was the first time she had heard Tre speak a complete sentence. It made her wonder if perhaps he understood everything they had been saying all along, but he was actually too shy to enter into the conversation.

It helped to see that side of Tre, because when she rode with him and Randy to the Highland House that afternoon, Sierra felt much more comfortable with Tre and more prepared to go at this project the second time as a team—even if Vicki hadn't been there practice with them.

Randy pulled up in front of the gated yard and parked. A dozen noisy kids spotted them climbing out of Randy's truck and ran to the gate to welcome them. Sierra smiled and greeted the kids as they all spoke at once. Some wanted to play baseball. Others begged for a round of soccer. Two little girls came running up and reminded Sierra that she had promised to do art with them.

"First we'll all go inside and have our meeting time," Sierra said. She looked over their heads, scanning the porch for any sight of Paul. "We have something really great planned for you today."

"I know what that is," one boy said to Randy. "You have a guitar."

"That's right," Randy said. "You want to come in and hear me play it?"

"Are you any good?" a kid asked.

"Not as good as Tre here."

All the kids turned their attention to Tre as they climbed the stairs to the front porch.

"Come on in, you guys." Sierra put her hand on the doorknob. "Wait until you see our surprise."

As she opened the door, Sierra stopped cold. Paul and Vicki stood there, only inches apart. Her face was tilted up toward his, and Paul was staring into her eyes, his right hand poised to stroke her cheek.

## chapter fifteen

THE TROOPS EXPLODED INTO THE ROOM, BUT neither Paul nor Vicki moved. The kids started to call out their snickering comments.

"He's going to kiss her!"

"Ooo! Puppy love!"

As Sierra and the others watched, Vicki blinked a few times, and Paul's fingers gently dabbed underneath her right eye.

"There," he said, holding up his index finger in front of Vicki. "Got it."

"Thanks!" Vicki said. "This new lens won't stay in. It slides to the corner, and I can't get it."

Paul didn't seem to listen to her. He had turned to look at the group, and the first person his gaze rested on was Sierra.

"Hi," she said above the rumble of the kids. Her two sidekicks were each tugging on an arm, urging her into the meeting room, where the director was leading the rest of the children.

"Hi," Paul said back. He wore a light-blue denim work

shirt with the sleeves rolled up. A braided leather bracelet circled his left wrist, and a carpenter's tool belt was wrapped around his middle. From it hung a hammer and tape measure.

"Vicki," Randy said, stepping in front of Sierra, nearly whacking her with the end of his guitar case. "You want to help us with the songs?"

Vicki held out the wayward contact on her finger. Sierra noticed Vicki now had one aqua-blue eye while the other eye showed her true color, a subtle gray. "I'll be right in as soon as I fix my contact."

"I'm glad you're here," Randy called after her as she exited down the hallway. He turned to Sierra and said, "We'd better get in there."

Sierra's helpful parasites gladly fell in line behind Randy, leading Sierra away from Paul. Angie, the smaller one with long, stringy bangs, grabbed Sierra's right arm. Meruka, the more aggressive one with missing front teeth, locked on to Sierra's left arm. They pulled Sierra, arms first, into the meeting room. Just as the doors were about to close behind her, Sierra turned and looked back at Paul, who stood his ground in the entryway with his arms folded across his chest. He wore an amused expression.

"Will you be around?" she asked.

He nodded.

"Good," was all she could think to say as her arms received another hasty yank, and the meeting room gobbled her up.

Randy was telling the kids they needed to sit and listen.

Most of them settled down. Sierra sat cross-legged on the floor between her adoring friends and did her best to hush the other kids as Randy extracted his guitar from the case and began to tune up. Sierra noticed Vicki slipping in the back door and standing in the corner with Tre.

*Where's Paul?* Sierra thought. *Is he going to come in, too?*

Randy plunged right into the first song, a common Sunday school number, familiar to most American kids. However, Sierra was the only one in the room who started to sing along on the chorus. Apparently, these kids had never heard this song before.

Randy sang a couple more songs, which he tried to teach to the kids. They seemed to pay more attention to Randy than they had to Sierra on Tuesday.

Instead of a Bible story, Randy told the kids how he had become a Christian. Briefly, he related his story, quoting several verses. He told them how he had grown up going to church and believing he would go to heaven when he died. Then one day when he was eight, the drawstring to his bathing trunks got caught in a pool filter, and Randy nearly drowned trying to free it. At that moment, he wanted to make sure he was going to heaven, so he asked Christ to forgive his sins and come into his life.

"Did an angel come rescue you?" one of the fascinated kids asked.

"No," Randy said, his crooked smile peeking out. "I wiggled out of my trunks and swam to the surface in my birthday suit."

The kids burst out laughing, and it was nearly impossible to get them to focus back on Randy's serious conclusion.

"You need to make sure you've turned your life over to God," he said, raising his voice. "God wants you to come to Him. Remember the story of the prodigal son?"

Sierra wondered if any of them were listening at all. "Shhh! Pay attention now." *How can they understand?* she thought as she tried to quiet them down. *Prodigal is not a word they use every day. Why didn't I pick a different story? These kids aren't old enough to understand a prodigal losing everything and ending up in a pigpen.*

"Okay," Randy said in a last-ditch effort to corral the kids back in, "I'm going to pray now. Will all of you please close your eyes? That's right. Close out everything that's going on around you, and let's talk to God."

He prayed earnestly, and as if he had all the time in the world, not bothered by the rowdiness of the kids. Sierra prayed silently along with him, her head bowed, her eyes closed.

"Before you leave," Randy said loudly as his prayer ended and the kids scrambled for the doors, "we want you to know that God loves you. He wants you to come to Him and be adopted into His family as His very own kids."

The doors burst open and out they flew.

"Time to do art," Meruka said, turning to Sierra with a grin that exposed the gap where her front teeth had been.

"You promised," Angie reminded her.

"Okay," Sierra said, rising to her feet and slipping an arm around each of them. "Let's first tell Randy what a great job he did. Great job, Randy!"

"Great job, Randy," the girls echoed.

He looked exhausted. "Do you think any of them were listening?"

"I was listening," Meruka said.

"Me, too," said Angie, swatting her long bangs out of her eyes.

"Good," Randy responded, smiling at them. He took his guitar from the case. "Here," he said, holding it out to Tre. "Why don't you go out onto the porch and wow them?"

Tre's face lit up as he gratefully accepted Randy's offer.

"Come on," the impatient artists said. "Let's go!"

"Okay, okay. We're on our way." Sierra steered them toward the doors. As soon as they were in the hallway, she looked for Paul. "Girls?" she asked softly. "Do you know that nice guy who was in the hall here earlier?"

"You mean Paul?" Meruka asked.

"Yes. Have you seen him around?"

"Why? Are you in love with him?"

A tiny voice deep inside the treasure chest of Sierra's heart chirped out, *Yes! Yes! A thousand times yes!* Sierra felt her cheeks turning flame red and, ignoring the incarcerated voice, she laughed lightly and said, "No, of course not."

# chapter sixteen

SIERRA SPENT THE NEXT HALF HOUR DIRECTING her group of eager artists, which had grown to 11 kids. She thought of several ideas for easy art projects: bead stringing, clay figurines, puppets, masks, even colored macaroni necklaces. The ideas grew, and she wondered if the Highland House offered a summer program for these kids and if they would want a volunteer art instructor. She also wondered if Paul would be gone the entire summer.

A sudden distinct odor wafted into the room. Sierra turned toward the door, and there stood Monte, a hopeful glimmer in his brown eyes. "Do you remember me?"

"Yes, I do. How are you, Monte?"

He looked pleased that she remembered his name. "Can I do a picture?"

"Sure. Why don't you join these guys?" Sierra directed him to a side table where two boys sat, trying to fold paper airplanes the way Sierra had shown them. "Do you want to make a paper airplane, Monte? Or do you want to color?"

The other two kids at the table started to argue over the few pieces of paper allotted to them, saying there wasn't enough for Monte. Sierra could hear two of the girls at the other table saying, "Don't let him sit next to you. He kicks."

"I know. And he stinks, too."

"Get out of here, Monte!" one of the kids said.

Sierra found herself holding her breath again, wishing for all the world this small room had a fan she could turn on. The stench was overwhelming. Monte stood between the two tables, looking to Sierra for an answer.

"Ah, actually, Monte, did you want to go outside and play soccer with the other kids?"

He shook his head. "I want to make a frog."

"A frog," Sierra repeated. "Let's see. You want to make a frog." She quickly scanned the room. The door and both windows were already open. It was as ventilated as it was going to get. "Why don't we move out to the porch," she suggested. "It's such a gorgeous evening. We can take all our things with us. Everyone grab something and let's go."

The kids were reluctant to follow her instructions. Some of them abandoned their art projects altogether. By the time they had regrouped on the porch, only seven artists and Monte remained.

But for Sierra, the decision to move was a good one. The calm evening breeze skipped across the wide, open porch carrying the faint scent of honeysuckle mixed with bus fumes from the busy street beyond the yard. A long line was already forming at the kitchen next door. Sierra remembered hearing that they fed an average of 150 people a night. They also offered space to 85 people a night, with the men sleeping in the annex and the women and children in the two upstairs floors of the Highland House.

It amazed Sierra how so many people seemed to appear out of nowhere to line up each night. Where did they come from? How did they end up here? Each of them had a story.

"Monte," she said, spreading out her armful of art supplies, "how old are you?"

"He's five," a girl answered. "I'm older than him."

"Where did you live before you came here?" Sierra asked.

"I don't know," he said, dropping down next to her and scrounging for a green crayon.

"Has the Highland House been able to find a job for your mom?"

"I don't know where my mom is," Monte said. "She left when I was a baby. My uncle takes care of me."

Sierra found she could neither hold her breath nor steel her heart against this kid any longer. "Come on, Monte. Let's see if we can make you a frog."

The cold reality of it all hit Sierra like a sledgehammer. These kids were real, and they didn't choose to be in this condition. Their problems weren't going to go away overnight. She realized the situation called for more than a quick four hours of trying to entertain some children to meet a class requirement. Sierra felt as if something inside her connected with the kids, and she was right where God wanted her to be, doing exactly what He had created her to do—make a frog with Monte.

"We need some round, buggy eyeballs," Sierra said, reaching for the scissors. "And some long, good jumpy legs. Did you know that God made frogs?"

"I know that story about the prince," Angie said. "He got turned into a frog, and the princess had to kiss him to turn him back into a prince."

"Right," Sierra said, smiling. "That's a good fairy tale, isn't it?"

"I would never kiss a frog," Meruka spouted, her tongue sticking out through her toothless gap. "Ewww!"

"Some people eat frogs," a little boy announced.

"I'd rather kiss one than eat one."

"Here, Monte." Sierra held out the two bulging eyeballs she had made. "Are you ready for these?"

"Have you ever kissed a frog, Missy Era?"

"Missy Era?"

"That's your name, isn't it?"

"Oh. Miss Sierra," she decoded with a smile. "You can call me Sierra."

"Have you ever kissed a frog, Sierra?"

The truth was, at 16, she had never kissed any guy—frog or prince. "No, I've never kissed a frog."

The little girls giggled.

Suddenly, from the roof overhanging the porch, they heard a clamor of heavy footsteps. Sierra looked up and noticed for the first time the ladder leaning against the front of the house. Clunky boots appeared on the top rung and steadily made their way down the ladder. The circle of artists all watched as a pair of jeans appeared on the ladder above the boots. Next came a carpenter's belt topped with a blue denim work shirt.

Sierra swallowed hard. Paul had been above them the whole time. He must have heard her comments. Landing on the ground and hoisting the ladder under his arm, Paul slowly looked up, and Sierra caught his engaging grin.

He looked right at her and said only one word as he hauled away the ladder: "Ribbit."

# chapter seventeen

A N AGELESS YET BRAND-NEW FAIRY TALE danced inside Sierra's imagination. Was Paul trying to tell her he was a prince in disguise? She had already guessed that.

Only a week or so ago, she would have felt dangerous and impulsive—qualities that had bothered her about herself. Now she felt useful and determined. She was sure that Paul had some interest in her—a curiosity if nothing else. It confirmed her daydream that an attraction existed between her and Paul, and it wasn't only her feelings.

Quietly humming to herself, Sierra helped each kid with his or her art project. Monte's frog turned out to be kind of distorted and silly looking. It didn't matter to him. He showed everyone, proudly boasting that Sierra had helped him.

She collected the crayons and bits of paper from the porch as the children began to leave. Every now and then she looked up, checking to see if Paul was around. She didn't want him to disappear this time.

The director came out onto the porch and shook

Sierra's hand, thanking her for coming. She pulled him aside from the three kids still coloring and asked if she could continue to volunteer.

"We'd love it," Mr. Mackenzie said. "You can see how much we need the help. My nephew speaks highly of you."

*Paul spoke highly of me?*

"I think very highly of Paul as well," Sierra said. "And Jeremy. My sister, Tawni, is dating Jeremy."

"Really!" Mr. Mackenzie had a gentle, engaging manner about him. "And is your sister here?"

"No. But we'd like to invite you and Paul to come some evening for dinner before he leaves for Scotland."

"He's told you, then."

"Actually, Tawni told me."

"We'll have to see about arranging a meeting in the next week since Paul is leaving a week from tomorrow. You knew that, didn't you?"

Sierra felt as if a load of bricks had been dumped on her stomach. "No. I didn't know he was leaving so soon." Sierra cleared her throat. "My mom said she'd call you. I'm sure we can arrange something before he leaves."

"Wonderful! It's delightful to know you, Sierra. You are welcome here anytime. Any amount of volunteering you would like to do would be greatly appreciated."

Sierra finished picking up the art mess. Most of the kids had gone. Her two faithful sidekicks, Meruka and Angie, eagerly helped her clean up. She could barely think straight with this new information about Paul marching across her brain.

"Are you going to come back tomorrow?" Meruka quizzed her.

"What? Oh. No, not tomorrow. I will come back another day. And maybe we can do some more art."

"Will you tell us some more stories with puppets?" said Angie.

"Well, maybe. Would you like that?"

Angie looked at Sierra with innocent eyes and nodded her head.

"Hey, Sierra," Randy called from the yard, "you about ready to go?"

"No!" she called out a little too urgently. She hadn't talked with Paul yet. "I need to put these things inside. I'll be a few minutes."

"We'll be waiting," Randy said.

Sierra scooped up the last scrap of paper and dashed into the house. Slipping the supplies back into the cupboard, she quickly tidied up the room and then took off to find Paul. She couldn't locate him anywhere.

*He said he would be around. And last Tuesday, what was it he had said when he touched my arm? Something about how we should talk.*

She took one last peek in the meeting room and gave up. If she would see Paul tonight—or ever again—it would have to be a God-thing. Gathering up her disappointment, Sierra walked to Randy's truck with long strides. She sat next to Tre, silently staring out the window all the way to the pizza place. The cloud of gloom hung over her while they ate.

Paul was leaving in a week. How could they have come

so far in seeing each other and being around each other for hours, and yet still be so far away from each other?

Randy got Tre to open up and talk a little about his family and his interest in music. Sierra ate one slice of pizza and wondered if Mom had called Paul's uncle yet to set a time for them to come to dinner. When Randy dropped her off, she couldn't wait to run inside and ask Mom.

"Wait up," Randy said, following Sierra up the steps to her front door. She had forgotten how Randy usually hung out at their house on Fridays. It was only 8:30. Of course he would want to come in. That didn't mean she had to entertain him.

"Sounds like the boys are in the family room," Sierra said to Randy as they stepped inside. She planned to find her mom and make some dinner plans.

"Hey," Randy said as she made a beeline up the stairs, "I didn't come in to see your brothers."

Sierra stopped and looked down at Randy. His head was tilted, his eyes questioning. With a hesitant hand, he flipped back his straight blond hair.

"I was hoping we could talk for a while," he said.

"Now?" Sierra realized how rude that must sound. Randy always had time to listen to her woes. How hard would it be for her to do the same for him? "I mean, can you wait just a minute?"

"Sure," Randy said, giving her a crooked grin. "I'll wait in the family room."

"Thanks," Sierra said and then took the rest of the stairs two at a time.

She found Mom in Granna Mae's room. They were playing a game of Scrabble.

"Mom," Sierra asked breathlessly, "you know our idea about inviting Mr. Mackenzie and Paul for dinner? Paul leaves for Scotland in a week. If we're going to invite them, we should do it tomorrow night because I have finals all next week."

"Take a breath, Lovey," Granna Mae said.

"I called him about an hour ago. We're all set for next Friday night," Mom responded.

Sierra lowered herself onto the edge of Granna Mae's bed. *Next Friday. A whole week, and I won't see him until the day before he leaves! I have to work out something else. Something more. I need a chance to tell Paul how I've prayed for him and find a way to let him know how I feel about him.*

"Help me out here, will you, Lovey? I have a *j*, and I can't figure out how to use it."

Sierra went over and stood behind Granna Mae, examining her letters and running the possible combinations through her head. They couldn't use the *j* this time, but Sierra managed to come up with "aft," and the *f* landed on a triple letter box. The game proceeded at an increased pace now that Sierra and Granna Mae were teamed up against Mom, the reigning champion of the house.

Forty minutes later, the scores were tallied. Mom won by seven points.

"I suppose I should check on the boys," Mom said, stretching. "It's past their bedtime."

The image of her brothers watching TV brought back

the memory of Randy. "Oh, no!" Sierra said, jumping up and running downstairs. She blasted into the family room and saw only her dad and her two brothers engrossed in the last five minutes of a video. "Where's Randy?"

"He left a little while ago," Dad said. "Is everything okay?"

"I hope so," Sierra said, charging out the front door and scanning the street for his truck. He was long gone.

Sierra tipped her face heavenward and whispered, "I'm sorry." Here she had been so upset about Paul disappearing and her not being able to talk with him, and then, without thinking, Sierra had disappeared on Randy when he said he wanted to talk with her.

The thought hit Sierra that perhaps her anticipation of talking with Paul was not mutual after all. Maybe Paul saw Sierra the way she saw Randy—a pleasant interruption. In the stillness of the dark, empty night, the tears came, bubbling up from someplace deep inside.

# chapter eighteen

"**M**Y LIFE IS FALLING APART," AMY SAID ON the phone early the next morning.

Sierra was hurrying to dress for work, and she didn't feel a boatload of sympathy for Amy. Sierra's own emotions over not talking to Paul and ignoring Randy had kept her tossing and turning all night. She was not in a good mood.

"We can't have our dinner tonight because my sister has the flu and my mother thinks it's not polite to invite people to your house if someone is sick."

"Your mother's probably right," Sierra said, shuddering at the thought of getting the flu right now. "This is an awfully intense week ahead, Amy. Maybe we should wait until school is out."

"I guess we'll have to. I'll call Drake and tell him. I'm hoping he'll suggest we all go out to eat instead."

"That would be fine with me," Sierra said. She felt a little guilty about how clammed up she had been during the pizza outing the night before. First Sierra had made sure Tre was invited, and then she had ended up being lost in her own dream world the whole time. It would be good to see Randy tonight and get everything back on track. She couldn't do anything about Paul but wait until dinner next Friday. Or try to see him sometime this week at the Highland House. But that didn't seem like a great place to talk. At least she could apologize to Randy and feel better about that relationship.

All day at work, Sierra fought a headache. She attributed it to not enough sleep, stress over finals, anxiety over seeing Paul, and maybe that all she had eaten for breakfast was a mushy, spotted banana. Even the daily pan of "burnt offering" cinnamon rolls on the table in the back offered no solace. Jody offered her a packet of Energy Revive, a collection of vitamin B and ginseng tablets. Sierra believed vitamins were a good thing. But the way her stomach was feeling, it didn't seem likely she would be able to keep the pills down.

The instant the round tummy of the bear clock on the wall announced that it was 4:00, Sierra was out of there. What a relief to know she could go straight home since Amy's dinner party had been postponed. None of Sierra's friends had contacted her at work, so she didn't know if they were planning on doing something. If they were, she decided she would pass. All she wanted was a hot bath, some food, and a long nap.

Her heart sank when she turned down the street and saw Randy's truck parked in front of her house. A large mower stuck out of the back of the truck bed. Randy stood in the front yard in his lawn service clothes, wearing

a blue baseball cap backward and talking to Sierra's dad.
They both heard the noisy approach of her diesel-engine
VW Rabbit and turned to watch her park. Both of them
smiled and waved.

Sierra wished she could vaporize and not have to go
through this humble apology to Randy. She knew he
would understand about her deserting him last night.
He always did. She just didn't like admitting she had forgotten about him.

"Hi," she called out, slamming the car door and
forcing her brightest smile.

"What? No leftovers for the family this week?" Dad
said, noticing she wasn't carrying the white bakery bag she
usually brought with her each Saturday evening.

"Didn't I tell you? Mrs. Kraus decided to start
donating all the extras to the Highland House."

"They need them more than we do," Dad said, patting
his stomach. "Well, I have a project going out back. I'll see
you around, Randy."

"'Bye," Randy said. Turning to Sierra, he cautiously
asked, "Are you doing okay?" He looked adorable in the
backward baseball cap with blond fringes of his floppy
hair sticking out of the sides. He smelled like freshly cut
grass, and his pants looked as if he had just lost a tackle
football game.

"I'm okay. Randy, I apologize about last night."

He didn't halt her painful admission but let her
continue.

"I don't know what to say. I meant to come down right

after I talked to my mom. But then I started helping
Granna Mae with her *j* in the Scrabble game, and I lost
track of time."

Instead of his usual amiable laugh and crooked smile
to show he understood, Randy's face remained still. Sierra
thought she saw a hint of hurt in his eyes.

"I knew it had to be something important," Randy said
with a bite to his words. "Look, Sierra. If you don't want
me to come around, just tell me. I thought we were getting
pretty close. You know—buddies. Now I'm not sure
what's going on. If I'm bugging you, I want you to tell me."

"You don't bug me, Randy. Not at all. Please don't
ever think that. It's just that . . ." She didn't know how to
tell him about her overwhelming feelings for Paul. He
would probably understand. Randy was such a good
listener, and he definitely kept confidences better than
Amy. Still, it felt odd telling one guy that she liked another
guy.

"What is it?" Randy said, adjusting his weight from
one foot to the other.

"There's been a lot going on lately. I know I've been
acting kind of strange. Please don't read anything into
that about our friendship. I need you to hang in there with
me for this next week or so."

Randy was quiet for a few moments, absorbing her
words. "I can do that," he said.

"Good. Thanks." Sierra smiled her relief at him.

"I guess our dinner at Amy's was canceled," he said. "I
thought I'd see if you wanted to go do something."

A little night-light next to Sierra's heart suddenly lit in a soft glow. He was actually asking her to go out. It was so sweet of him. "I was planning to come home and crash," Sierra said. "I'm fried, and I still have to type up the written report for the Highland House. If you want to stay for dinner, I'm sure it would be fine with my parents."

Randy seemed to weigh the options. "I think I'll follow your shining example," he said, the comforting, crooked grin creeping back into place. "I should go home and finish my report, too. Maybe we can do something next weekend—just the two of us—after the pressure of finals is off. How about Friday night?"

"Sure," Sierra said quickly. It felt good to have things cleared up with Randy. He turned to leave, and then she remembered. Friday was when Paul and his uncle were coming for dinner. "Ah, maybe not Friday. We have company coming. You and I could do something on Saturday, couldn't we?"

"Saturday," Randy repeated, as if trying to verbally stick a thumbtack in Sierra's words to get them to stay in one place. "I think there's a concert Saturday night."

"Great! That would be fun. See you Monday." She waved good-bye and made her way to the bathtub.

When Sierra did see Randy on Monday, it was right before they were to give their reports in front of the class.

"You go first," he said, then added teasingly, "we'll save the best for last."

Sierra stood before Mr. Rykert's class and gave her presentation, feeling at ease in front of the group. Public speaking didn't spook her the way it did a lot of her friends.

Coming to a conclusion, Sierra said, "For me, the best part about going to the Highland House was discovering we can do lots of things to fulfill the commandment of Christ found in Luke 6:31." She looked down at her note cards and read, "'Do to others as you would have them do to you.'"

Looking at her classmates, Sierra said, "Whether it's donating time or food or assistance of some kind, lots of needs are out there, and there's plenty we can do about them. I plan to continue to volunteer at the Highland House. I'd like to close with a verse from Matthew 25:37–40. 'Then the righteous will answer him, "Lord, when did we see you hungry and feed you, or thirsty and give you something to drink? When did we see you a stranger and invite you in, or needing clothes and clothe you? When did we see you sick or in prison and go to visit you?" The King will reply, "I tell you the truth, whatever you did for one of the least of these brothers of mine, you did for me."'"

Sierra had begun her report telling about Monte and his paper frog. She concluded by saying, "Perhaps Monte would be considered one of the least of these. I learned that in serving Monte, I'm actually serving Christ."

Before she could take her seat, the class burst into applause. Randy stood up, clapping and whistling. Sierra turned and swatted her hand in his direction to get him to sit down and stop making such a ruckus. She had to admit, though, she did like the way Randy teased her.

"Wonderfully presented, Sierra," Mr. Rykert said, walking to the front of the class. "We'll hear now from Tre." He nodded at Tre, urging him to go up front.

Sierra's heart went out to Tre. He was perspiring and looked as if he would rather have his toenails lit on fire than have to stand in front of everyone.

"I went to the Highland House," he began, trembling and swallowing hard. "I helped with the children, and I played the guitar. I learned about the prodigal son."

He seemed to have difficulty saying "prodigal," and once again Sierra wished she hadn't picked that story. It was certainly too difficult for the children to understand.

"I know about the pigs," Tre continued. A ripple of laughter moved through the classroom. "I don't want to have that life, so I made a choice at the Highland House to come back to the Father God, who is waiting for me."

It was completely still for a moment, as everyone tried to absorb what he had said.

Mr. Rykert stepped closer to Tre and said, "Are you saying you made a decision to turn your life over to God?"

Tre nodded. His expression seemed to relax as he said, "My friends showed me Jesus." Glancing first at Sierra and then at Randy, he added, "And I wanted to know Him, too."

Sierra looked over her shoulder at Randy. His mouth was open, and his eyes crinkled in surprise. Turning back to meet Tre's gaze, Sierra felt the tears rushing to her eyes, demanding to be released.

*Tre a Christian?! The prodigal story and those silly pigs made sense to him? I don't believe it. What a God-thing!*

Mr. Rykert appeared to be choked up. He stood beside Tre and placed his hand on the boy's shoulder. "I'd like to pray for you, son." And pray he did—rich, meaningful words of thanks to God.

The dismissal bell rang before Mr. Rykert finished praying. Everyone waited. Mr. Rykert said, "Amen." Instead of rushing out of the class, most of the students went up front to say something to Tre. He seemed surprised and a bit confused by all the attention.

"That was close," Vicki said as she, Amy, and Sierra exited the room. "I was supposed to give my report after Tre. How do you follow that?"

"He didn't say all that just to get a good grade," Amy said.

"I know," Vicki said. "I was making a little joke. Relax." She turned to Sierra and said, "Are you and Randy going to the Sierra concert on Saturday?"

"You got that sentence mixed up," Amy corrected her. "You mean, 'Are you going to the concert on Saturday, Sierra?'"

"Amy, the name of the group is 'Sierra.' You knew that, didn't you?"

"No!"

"Neither did I," Sierra said. "How fun! I'm definitely going. Randy said something about it, but I'd love to go even if he doesn't want to. Do you want to go with us, Amy?"

"I'm supposed to start working at my uncle's on Saturday. And what about our lobster dinner?" Amy said with a pout. "Weren't we going to move that back a week?"

"How about moving it back two weeks?" Sierra suggested. "I'd really like to go to this concert."

"I have extra tickets if you want to buy one from me," Vicki said. "I'm going with Mike. You and Randy can double with us if you want."

For the first time, it hit Sierra that other people thought of her and Randy as a couple, not just buddies. She wasn't sure how she felt about that.

# chapter nineteen

MOM MADE MEAT LOAF FOR THE FRIDAY night dinner, and the house filled with the scent of it baking alongside a dozen fat potatoes. Salad, green beans, homemade soda bread, and an apple crisp with vanilla ice cream completed the menu. In Sierra's opinion, it was perfect.

At 5:30, Sierra was still deciding what to wear. This was probably the biggest wardrobe decision she had ever had to make. And for the first time, Tawni seemed to understand what Sierra was going through.

"I think you should wear the skirt with the embroidered vest," Tawni said. "It's a nice, soft look, but not out of character for you."

"I don't know," Sierra said, eyeing the five potential outfits laid out on her bed. "That's what I had on the day he saw me walking home in the rain with the armful of daffodils. I looked like a drowned rat," Sierra said.

"Is that why Jeremy says Paul calls you the Daffodil Queen?"

Sierra nodded, remembering only too well the teasing

letter Paul had sent her after that frustrating experience. "Are you sure this gauze dress wouldn't be better?" She held up a long, cream-colored peasant dress. "With lots of beads?"

Tawni shook her head. "You look better with a little color by your face. That gauze dress looks like a night-gown. Trust me. Go with the vest and skirt. You can still wear all your little beads with that if you want."

Sierra gave in, knowing her sister was right. This was probably her favorite outfit of the batch.

Tawni wore a light-blue skirt and jacket, which she had worn to work that morning. Today had been her last day. Her transfer went through to the San Diego Nordstrom, and she would be moving within a week—two weeks at the most. The crazy thing was, for the first time in their lives, Tawni and Sierra were enjoying each other's company. Tawni had even invited Sierra to drive down to Southern California with her and then fly home. Sierra had put off deciding, saying she wanted to make it through finals week and this dinner with Paul.

Finally, Friday was here. No more papers or reports. Only one more final next week, and then she would be done. In a few minutes, Paul would be in her house, and she would be looking into his eyes. Somehow she would find a way to talk privately with him, and she would tell him how much she cared for him, how intensely she had prayed for him. And then . . .

Sierra didn't know what would happen then. Maybe they would write letters all summer. Maybe there would be a few overseas phone calls. When he returned in the fall, she would be 17 and a senior. Paul wouldn't—couldn't—consider her too young then.

Slipping on the last bracelet and flopping a handful of curly hair over her shoulder, Sierra took one last look in the antique oval dresser mirror to make sure she hadn't messed up Tawni's expert makeup job. The mascara on her lashes was barely noticeable. She had let Tawni put makeup on her only once before. It was the first night Randy had come over. Even on that "first date," Sierra had been thinking of Paul and wishing he were the one coming to her front door instead of Randy. Tonight her wish was coming true.

Lightly taking the stairs down to the kitchen, Sierra smiled. She imagined she was glowing. Funny how much more understanding she now had for Tawni and her excitement over Jeremy. It only made the intrigue more inviting knowing that Jeremy and Paul were brothers. Sierra and Tawni now had so much more to share as sisters.

Just as she fluttered off the last stair, the doorbell rang. Sierra rushed to the door, then stopped and closed her eyes, drawing in a deep breath before opening the door to their evening guests.

"Randy!" she sputtered.

"Hey, you look nice," Randy said. Then, with a flash of recollection, he thumped his forehead with the palm of his hand and said, "Oh, yeah, you guys have company tonight."

Just then a car pulled up and parked across the street. Sierra bit her lower lip and tried to think fast.

"Is that them?" Randy said, peering at the guy who emerged from the car wearing jeans and a long-sleeved white shirt. His dark, wavy brown hair was combed off his broad forehead, and in his hand he held a small bouquet of daffodils. Sierra thought her heart was going to jump right out of her skin and go hopping down the front steps to greet him.

"Hey, isn't that Paul?" Randy said. "He's your company?" Randy's face took on that twinge of hurt.

"And his uncle," Sierra said quickly. "Mr. Mackenzie. Tawni's boyfriend is Paul's brother."

"Is that right? I didn't know that. Hey, Paul." Randy greeted him with a hearty handshake. "How's it going?" He looked behind him and said, "Isn't your uncle coming?"

"He sends his apologies," Paul said politely, looking at Sierra. "He was short on volunteers tonight to serve dinner at the Highland House. I hope it's okay that I still came."

"Of course!" Sierra said, eyeing the sweet bouquet.

"These are for Granna Mae," he said, holding them out.

"Oh, yes. Of course they are. Come on in." Sierra took the daffodils and held the door open for Paul. Randy followed him inside. Sierra swallowed hard, not sure what to do. This would not be the night of her dreams if Randy stayed for dinner, too. And of course he would be invited to stay since a place was already set for Mr. Mackenzie.

Sierra considered pulling Randy into the study and confiding her deepest dreams and hopes to him. Surely, he would understand what a special night this was, and he would graciously leave. Randy would do that for her. She knew he would. If only she could figure out a way to tell him so it wouldn't hurt his feelings. He seemed to be wearing them on his sleeve lately.

"Short on volunteers," Randy said. "I'd be glad to help. Do you think if I went down there, your uncle would be able to come here for dinner?"

Sierra felt like giving Randy a big hug for being so sweet and sensitive to the situation. And she didn't have to say anything. What a great guy! *Now, go, Randy. Go.*

"I'm sure he would appreciate the break," Paul said. "Thanks, Randy." Then, flashing a glance from Sierra to Randy as if trying to detect the relationship between the two of them, Paul added, "That would be great."

"Cool," Randy said. "I'll see you guys later." He looked at Sierra a little longer than necessary, and she wondered if Randy was doing the same thing as Paul, trying to pick up hidden signals.

"Thanks, Randy," Sierra said, smiling warmly, but not too warmly. All her best smiles had been saved for Paul. As soon as Randy turned away, Sierra took her best smile out and hung it from her perfect lips like a welcome sign meant only for Paul.

## chapter twenty

*P*AUL MADE A BIG HIT WITH SIERRA'S FAMILY, especially with Tawni, who kept saying, "You looked just like Jeremy when you said that."

"Uncle Mac," as Paul called his uncle, arrived right as they were sitting down in the large dining room. He couldn't stop praising Randy, who had come to his rescue. Uncle Mac sat next to Paul, who was seated directly across from Sierra. When her dad motioned for them to hold hands while he prayed, Sierra closed her eyes and wished for all the world she were sitting next to Paul instead of Gavin and Tawni. Then it would be Paul's strong hand she was slipping hers into.

Several times during dinner, Sierra glanced up and thought she caught Paul looking at her. He always looked away, of course. Sierra couldn't wait until she had a chance to talk with him alone. She still didn't know how that would work out.

Granna Mae certainly didn't hide her affection for the young man. She loved the bouquet of "daffies" he brought her and had placed them in the center of the table.

Mom and Tawni were serving the apple crisp when Paul turned to Sierra's dad and quietly said, "I'd like to ask a favor. Actually, Jeremy asked me to do this as a favor for him."

"Sure," Dad said agreeably, without even knowing what it was.

"Would it be all right with you if I took Tawni and Sierra out for coffee after dinner?"

Sierra felt her heart immediately take an express elevator up to her throat. What a quaint "courting" approach. She loved it.

"It's fine with me if it's fine with them."

Paul looked at Sierra first. She somehow found the composure to suppress her ricocheting emotions and simply smile with a nod. Tawni kept serving, but a mischievous grin seemed to dance across her face.

The grin remained as the three of them drove off an hour later, heading for downtown Portland.

"Any place in particular?" Paul asked. "Jeremy said you had a place in mind."

Tawni directed Paul across the Burnside Bridge and into the West Portland hills to a tiny coffee shop. They parked on a hill and took a seat inside, at a small, round table by the front window where happy red geraniums spilled from the wooden flower box. Only a few other customers gathered in the quiet shop. Sierra felt as if they had been transported to another country.

"You know what?" Tawni said. Sierra and Paul were seated, but Tawni was still standing. "A couple of shops are still open down the street, and I might not get back over here before I move. So, why don't you two go ahead. I'll be back in a bit."

She disappeared out the door. Sierra was looking down at the place mat, her hands clutching each other under the table. "I think we've been set up," she said quietly.

Paul didn't answer, waiting for her to look up and catch his gaze. "It appears so," he said. "Would you like something to drink?"

"Do you suppose a place like this has herbal teas?" Sierra asked.

"We can find out." Paul lifted two fingers and motioned for the waiter.

In that moment, with Paul's profile to fill her view, the rich aroma of coffee filling the air, and the mustached waiter approaching them, Sierra believed this was a dream. A lovely jaunt to Paris for a cup of java on the Champs-Élysées. Only, in this dream, her eyes were open. She didn't want to close them for fear it would all vanish.

"Yes, one Black Forest," Paul said, "and do you have herbal tea?"

The waiter nodded and returned to the coffee bar.

"Did you want biscotti or anything?" Paul asked.

She was pretty sure he was referring to those long, hard cookies she had seen her parents dunk in their coffee. "No, I'm still full from dinner."

"Me, too. That was great. You have a wonderful family," Paul said. "Everything Jeremy said was true."

"Oh? And what did Jeremy tell you?"

"Well," Paul said, leaning back, "he said you're a pretty good surfer."

Sierra smiled.

"He also said you're a strong-hearted individual. But I could have told him that."

The waiter returned with a glass mug of coffee for Paul and a round, white teapot with a mug that fit on top. He presented Sierra with a basket of herbal tea bags for her to select from.

"Oh, and do you have any honey?" Sierra asked as the waiter turned to go.

"Jeremy also told me you're quite a prayer warrior."

Sierra felt this was the opportunity she had been waiting for. She dipped her tea bag of wild blackberry tea into the white pot and gathered her practiced phrases. Then she made them all line up and wait on the edge of her lips until the waiter placed the honey in front of her and left.

"What's that phrase? 'The warrior is a child'?" Paul sipped his coffee and looked at Sierra with an expression she recognized only too well. It was the same way Wesley looked at her. An invisible pat on the head. The endearing look big brothers bestow on kid sisters when they do something cute.

The world seemed to stop. It was as if her breath had suddenly been punched out of her lungs. *He thinks I'm a kid—a punky, little kid. He's not thinking any of the romantic things I'm thinking about him.*

This changed everything. No way could she pour out

her heart to this guy and tell him how hard and how long she had done battle for him. He wouldn't care that she had begged God to bring Paul back to Himself when he was wandering off.

"My brother also tells me," Paul paused, a compassionate smile lingering on his lips, "that you have a crush on me."

Now Sierra could barely move. She felt her face heat up like a Roman candle about to explode. Her breath came back, rapid and sharp.

*A crush on you! Is that what you think this is? Me in some puppy-love phase of my young life and you the master, oh so mature and wise? Of all the nerve!*

Now she really didn't know what to say. Why did Tawni leave her? Had she set this up? Were Tawni and Jeremy trying to make fun of her?

Resisting the impulse to stand up and dump the table in Paul's lap, Sierra stared at her hands and made herself prepare her cup of tea. She went about the task slowly, giving herself time to calm down and respond to Paul in a way she could live with. This was one time she refused to react impulsively, which would only prove his assumptions of her immaturity.

Paul waited quietly, his hands wrapped around his half-full glass mug.

"You know . . . ," Sierra said, setting down her spoon and taking a sip of her hot tea. Paul seemed to be hanging on to her words, waiting for her response. As sweet and mature as could be, Sierra said, "I think God brings different relationships into our lives at different times to teach us different things." She wanted it to sound profound. It ended up sounding redundant.

After another sip, she continued, finally looking up, allowing him to see into her tearless eyes. "I wonder if perhaps God brought you and me together for one brief season so that I could learn how God really does answer prayer."

Paul seemed startled by her response. He had looked at her like this before at the airport in London. This obviously was not what he expected her to say.

"You're a lot closer to the Lord than you were when we first met," Sierra suggested.

"Yes," Paul said with a nod.

"And you're off to Scotland now for the summer to help at your grandfather's mission. That's a different direction than you were headed last January."

Again Paul had to agree. "I'm going for a year," he corrected her. "Not just for the summer. I'll be going to a university in Edinburgh."

Something pinched and twisted inside Sierra. Even though he had cut her down to size with his "puppy-love" insinuations, the news still touched her somewhere deep inside. Going away for the summer was very different from going away for a year.

"I hope it goes well for you," Sierra said, dredging up one of the smiles she had been reserving for Paul only. "I'm just glad our paths crossed when they did." She was going to add something about them now traveling in different orbits, but it sounded too much like Amy's sci-fi psychology.

Leaning forward, Sierra was the one to lightly tap Paul's forearm this time. Looking through his eyes, right into his soul, she said in a whisper, "God has His mark on you, Paul Mackenzie. He's going to do something incredible in your life."

Paul didn't move. He continued to hold Sierra's gaze. "Thank you," he said, his voice low and husky. The earlier smirking look he wore seemed to have evaporated. "And thanks, too, for all your prayers. Don't stop."

Sierra paused before making her promise back to him. She took this seriously, whether he did or not. Was she willing to keep praying for him no matter where he lived, no matter whom he married, no matter what he did, no matter if she ever saw him again in her life? And would she be true to that promise knowing that the emotional connection she had felt with Paul was apparently one-sided?

"Okay," Sierra agreed, still holding his gaze. "I'll keep praying for you."

# chapter twenty-one

SIERRA TOSSED AND TURNED IN HER BED. SHE had barely slept all night. She and Tawni had talked until after midnight, trying to figure out the evening. Tawni admitted she and Jeremy had rigged the meeting, but they had hoped it would allow Paul and Sierra a chance to open their hearts to each other and see what would happen.

As Sierra saw it, she was glad she hadn't opened her heart because Paul had made it clear he wasn't interested in her. Certainly not the same way she had become so preoccupied with thoughts of him.

That realization had hurt something within Sierra, something she hadn't even known existed—a deep well of emotions from which she would have been only too willing to draw, if only Paul had asked. But he hadn't.

So, instead of those intense, womanly emotions having a chance to spring up, Sierra had capped them. She was fiercely embarrassed by having misread Paul's previous signals: his pithy letters, the way he seemed to have gazed into her eyes more than once, as if searching for his own reflection there, even his humorous "Ribbit" at the Highland House. None of these communications was intended to say anything especially personal.

Paul hadn't given her any more hints of his interest during their final hour together. He had finished his coffee; she had finished her tea. He paid the bill, and then they went outside into the spring drizzle. They stood close but silent in the glow of the antique streetlight under the café's blue-striped canopy.

Sierra noticed the geraniums and said absent-mindedly, "Those are Martha Washingtons. The geraniums, I mean. They're my mom's favorite."

Paul had nodded pleasantly.

Sierra felt miserably ridiculous talking about stupid flowers. Here she had thought a whole world was open to her and Paul, when in actuality, there was nothing.

Tawni arrived and got in the car with them, jabbering about the great deal she had found on her favorite lipstick. They had driven home.

Paul walked them both to the door, and Tawni wrapped her arms around his neck in a hug.

"Have a great time in Scotland," she said. "I'm so glad I got to meet you before you left."

"I hope it's a wonderful year for you," Sierra agreed, managing one more smile for him. "Good-bye, Paul."

"Good-bye," Paul said. "God bless."

With a final look into Sierra's eyes under the porch light, Paul turned and took long-legged strides to his car. He started the engine and pulled away from the curb. That was it. He was gone. Out of her life forever.

As Sierra and Tawni hashed it all out in their beds with the lights turned low, Sierra surmised a neat and convenient spiritual conclusion as to why their paths had crossed. She told Tawni what she had said to Paul, that they were brought together for a season and because of that, she had learned how to pray consistently for someone. More than that—to do spiritual battle for him. Sierra insisted, quite unemotionally, that it was a lesson well worth learning.

Tawni apologized, saying she never would have imagined things would go the way they did. In her mind, Tawni had believed all kinds of potential existed for a long-distance relationship between Sierra and Paul. It had worked for Tawni and Jeremy; why shouldn't it work for Sierra and Paul? It just didn't.

The illuminated clock face read 5:27. Quietly rising, Sierra tucked her feet into her bunny slippers and grabbed her Bible and journal. She padded softly to the library downstairs and began to pray for Paul, asking God to protect him as he was preparing to leave in a few hours for Scotland.

Then, opening her Bible, Sierra noticed a bookmark she had picked up at the Christian bookstore the last time she had stopped by. It quoted a verse from 2 Corinthians: "He puts a little heaven in our hearts so that we'll never settle for less."

"That's what it is," Sierra wrote in her journal. "I want God's kingdom to come and His will to be done on earth as it is in heaven. I desire God's best. At least I think I do—I want to. So, in my heart, I hold all these treasures. They're bits of heaven, and I won't settle for less. I don't know exactly how this applies to Paul, but I want God's best for him, and I hated seeing him settle for so much less."

She took a deep breath and continued writing. "That season is over. The season of wondering if he felt anything for me the way I felt so deeply for him. He's gone. I release this whole relationship to You, Father. Please don't let me ever settle for anything less than Your best."

Now she was the one who felt like the prodigal. She had given in to runaway dreams with Paul, and they had taken her nowhere. She was back in her heavenly Father's arms now—a safe place to be. Isn't that what it said on the Highland House sign? She tried hard to remember and then wrote the words in her journal. "A safe place for a fresh start." Sierra read the phrase again and then added, " . . . in my heavenly Father's arms."

Sierra felt strangely calm and at peace all day at work. Randy stopped by and told her how much fun he had had serving dinner at the Highland House the night before. She thanked him again for filling in for Uncle Mac.

"No need to thank me. I had a great time. Let's go back there together sometime," Randy suggested. "I'd like to keep helping out."

"I would, too," Sierra agreed.

"Do you want me to pick you up for the concert tonight?"

Once again Sierra had forgotten she had made social plans. She was really tired, but she had been looking forward to hearing this group. "Sure. Do you want to see if Vicki and Mike want to ride with us?"

"I already asked Mike. He said they're going out to eat first, so I told him we would meet them in front of the auditorium. A bunch of other people from school are going."

"Sounds like it will be great," Sierra said, feeling a little revived after her emotionally draining night. "I'll see you at my house later."

"Cool. I'll be there at 6:30."

Sierra wasn't ready when he arrived. She had given in to a little snooze after coming home from work. Mom woke her, saying that Randy was downstairs eating dinner with them, and he said they were supposed to go to a concert.

Springing from her bed and rattling off the details to Mom as she quickly changed into a clean T-shirt, Sierra pulled herself together. Fifteen minutes later, she and Randy were on their way to the concert. The inside of his truck smelled of cut grass and mud. She was glad she had worn old jeans in case she picked up some grass stains from the seat.

The parking lot was jam-packed, and they had to park, as Randy said, "in Outer Mongolia."

"I told Mike we would meet them at the front door," Randy said as they jogged to the front of the arena.

The marquee above them announced in huge letters,

"Tonight in concert SIERRA." It gave her a little smile to see her name in lights like that.

They searched the thinning crowd for Mike and Vicki but didn't see them.

"I'll go inside," Randy said. "You want to wait here a few more minutes in case they're late?"

"How will I find you?" Sierra asked, sticking her hand in her back jeans pocket, making sure she still had her ticket.

"I'll be back," he said, taking off without further instructions.

Sierra felt a slight sense of loss as he hurried away. She noticed he was dressed nicer than usual. He had even brought her a tiny clump of wild violets, which she had hastily tossed on the kitchen counter as they were blasting out the door. She wondered if he was trying to compete with Paul's bouquet for Granna Mae, but Randy's explanation had been that he saw them while mowing a lawn and didn't have the heart to mow them down.

Watching, waiting, tapping her foot, Sierra began to feel nervous as the final few concertgoers hurried in the front door. Surely it had already started, and she was missing it. It wouldn't be that difficult to find Randy inside. Vicki and Mike had to be in there already.

She turned in her ticket and slid through the door. Muffled cheers rose from behind the closed auditorium doors.

*So, what do I do? Stand around out here or go inside?*

She opted for going in. The auditorium was packed.

People stood, applauding, and Sierra knew she had already missed the first song. Now she was irritated. True, it was her fault they were late, but why had Randy left her? She would never find him now. Slipping into an empty aisle seat next to a row of strangers, Sierra decided she could enjoy the concert and watch for Randy at the same time from this vantage point. If nothing else, she would have time alone to think, to finish processing her thoughts about Paul before locking them away forever.

A spotlight hit the center stage. Three young women appeared, each with a microphone in hand. Their mellow voices blended, filling the auditorium with a song about trusting God. Sierra immediately knew she was going to like this group. Their music could soothe her soul and keep her company as she privately sorted out her life. This was exactly what she needed tonight.

# chapter twenty-two

A S SIERRA LISTENED TO THE NEXT UPBEAT
song, she felt as if all the pieces were falling
into place. The lyrics of peace and hope
toned down her spiritual evaluations over Paul and
soothed her emotions. She began to relax.

She watched for Randy but didn't see him. She knew
he would understand why she had come inside. Randy
was always understanding—understanding and patient.
And he was kind and considerate of her as well. As a
matter of fact, Randy was pretty terrific.

Thinking back on how he had handled the kids at the
Highland House, Sierra found herself smiling. Randy
was right. The two of them did make a great team. He will-
ingly put up with her teasing—like that day at Lotsa Tacos
when she grabbed his money.

Sierra realized he was the kind of guy she got along with
best: someone who let her be herself, yet didn't let her
dominate.

The song came to a velvety close as the trio harmo-
niously blended, drawing out the last note like a single

breath. The auditorium exploded in applause, and the blond singer in the middle stepped forward to recapture the audience's attention.

"I'm Wendi Foy Green," she said. "And I'd like you to meet Deborah Schnelle and Jennifer Hendrix. We're Sierra."

More applause thundered from the enthusiastic audience.

"Over the past few years as we've been singing together," Wendi said as the crowd hushed, "we've learned a lot about friendships. As with any relationship, there can be difficulties and misunderstandings. We truly believe we have to hold on to real love, which is Jesus, because He's the only One who can keep us together."

A guitarist began to strum in the background as Wendi said, "I wrote this song with my friend Connie. We had that kind of love in mind."

Wendi looked at Deborah and Jennifer and began to sing:

> We've had our moments;
> Some are better than the rest.
> And sometimes our devotion
> Gets put to the test.
> But we can stay together
> Through the darkest times,
> If we decide that love's
> The anchor of our lives.

> Hold on to Love
> 'Cause it's the only thing worth holding on to.
> Hold on to Love,
> And when it's all been said and done,
> We'll find that Love's the One
> That's holding on to us.
>
> I say I need you,
> And you say you need me, too.
> But if our hearts get torn,
> There's mending we must do.
> 'Cause we can't take for granted
> The love we've come to know.
> We've got to fan the flame
> If it's ever gonna grow.

A large screen behind the singers' heads ran a black-and-white video of the group as the sax played a soothing interlude. The video showed an interesting mix of hands—hands folded in prayer, fingers moving over a page of Braille, a baby's hand grasping his mother's finger, and a hand reaching over to grasp the hand of a friend.

Looking around for Randy, Sierra felt her heart beating faster as the group sang the chorus again.

> Hold on to Love
> 'Cause it's the only thing worth holding on to.
> Hold on to Love,
> And when it's all been said and done,

We'll find that Love's the One
That's holding on to us.

Sierra stepped into the aisle as the applause rose around her. Everything inside her told her to run out of there and find Randy. Maybe she was a little slow at this dating thing—"a late bloomer," as Tawni once called her. Maybe she didn't know a good thing when it was right in front of her nose. Randy had been there for her all along, bringing her a rose before his big date with Vicki, volunteering to fill in for Uncle Mac, and even thinking of Sierra when he pulled up that endangered clump of wild violets.

Why hadn't she seen it before? Amy was right all along. Sierra had been too absorbed in her dream of Paul to pay attention to the true friendship she already had with Randy.

Dashing into the lobby, Sierra scanned the area, hoping Randy might be there looking for her. She didn't see him. Then, out of the corner of her eye, she noticed a lone figure standing outside the front of the auditorium, right where he had left her.

*That couldn't be Randy! Could it?*

Sierra pushed open the glass door and ran into the cool evening air. "Randy! Over here, Randy!"

He turned, and when he saw her, a look of relief spread across his face. Jogging toward each other, they met halfway, both spouting explanations at the same time.

Impulsively and wholeheartedly, Sierra threw her arms around Randy and hugged him. When she pulled away,

Randy looked wonderfully surprised.

"You okay?" he asked, apparently trying to read her expression.

Sierra started to laugh, and with the laughter came unexpected tears cascading down her cheeks. She couldn't speak.

"Hey, what's wrong?" Randy didn't seem to know what to do with her. He stood awkwardly to the side, tilting his head and waiting for her to say something.

"Randy," she said, finally finding her voice, "I . . ." She brushed away her tears and felt all fresh and new inside. "I wanted to thank you for being my friend and for just being who you are. I think you're a wonderful person."

Randy looked at her as his crooked grin spread across his face. "Did you just figure that out?"

Sierra laughed again. She knew she didn't have to explain anything to him, nor would he ask her to. This is where she wanted to be. Right here, right now, with her buddy Randy.

"Do you want to go back inside?" he asked.

Sierra nodded and brushed away the last tears clinging to her eyelashes.

They turned to go, and Randy wrapped his big, rough hand around Sierra's and gave it a warm squeeze. She returned the squeeze, feeling a little bit of heaven in her heart.

Then, closing her eyes, Sierra made a wish that she would never settle for anything less than God's best for her.

*Devotion* is a word we hardly hear anymore. It combines the utmost dedication to something with a tender affection for that same thing. You can be devoted to a craft, a cause, or someone you love. In the case of the three effervescent young women of Sierra, that devotion encompasses all of those elements. For Wendi Foy Green, Jennifer Hendrix, and Deborah Schnelle, devotion means a wholehearted, energetic commitment to their music, their friends and families, and, most important, their Lord.

Devotion to the friendship these three women share is most obvious when one sees the group in concert—but sisterly harmony extends beyond the music. They have been around each other nearly every day for the last year and, according to Jennifer Hendrix, "they really are like my sisters; we share everything. It's been a real blessing just to be with them. And it's a lot of fun." As well as the three of them getting along, there are always going to be times when they have misunderstandings . . . the same goes for marriages and family relationships. It's then that they have to hold on to the real love—to Jesus. He's the only one who can give them all they need.

The songs from their recent release *Devotion* emphasize that reliance on the Lord. This album concentrates on the vertical relationship with God. Musically and lyrically, the songs of *Devotion* exemplify the nature of a rich relationship with God, from the exuberance of "I've Got the Joy" and "I Need" to the tenderness of "That's When I Find You" and "I Know You Know." But the vertical emphasis of these songs also serves to reinforce what the women of Sierra have learned along the way in talking with many new friends who come to Sierra concerts.

Back when they were practicing three-part harmony during lunch hours at Deborah's office, these three women had no idea what they were in for. But they devoted themselves to their craft in the hope of being able to share their songs, for the pure joy of musically expressing a vibrant faith. Though their success has surpassed all expectations, Wendi, Jennifer, and Deborah remain committed to the important things: their pastor and church, their own personal growth in the faith, and their relationships with family and friends—including all the new friends who have taken Sierra's music and message to their hearts.

It's the kind of thing you might call . . . devotion.